The Frightened Ones

By Melba Marlett

The Frightened Ones
Death Is in the Garden
Tomorrow Will Be Monday
Escape While I Can
Another Day Toward Dying
The Devil Builds a Chapel
Death Has a Thousand Doors

The Frightened Ones

Five Stories by Melba Marlett

WILDSIDE PRESS

Contents

The Frightened Ones	9
Second Chance	78
The Purring Countess	101
A Matter of Record	123
In Name Only	151

The Frightened Ones

The Frightened Ones

The man in gray crossed the bleak November fields running low, keeping out of sight of the road. Few trees grew in the sandy northern Michigan soil, but there was an occasional heap of underbrush or a straggling hedgerow, and under cover of these he rested, panting, eyeing the gray sky, estimating the length of time until twilight. Darkness had always been his element and he would welcome it now.

He cursed the roughness of the frozen earth and the clumsiness of his feet in their heavy prison shoes. Somewhere, somehow, he must get a car, and that would be very difficult. He dared not venture into a town, and casual motorists were almost non-existent in winter on these northern roads. The vision of his own two Cadillacs, hidden away in a Chicago garage, rose up before him, and he cursed again at the prospect of being at the mercy of some junk heap belonging to a backwoods farmer. Like any criminal, he detested lack of quality in the belongings of his victims.

Scrambling to the top of a small hill, he threw himself

on his stomach to look around. The only trace of human habitation in sight was a small house and a neat barn half a mile away. His sharp black eyes noted that no electric or telephone wires ran to the house. The poor boobs wouldn't have much, but maybe he could get a change of clothing there, something to cover up the Prison Farm stamping on the back of his shirt. There might be a little money lying around too, and he could be a long way off with it before one of the hicks could plod into town to give the alarm.

Half sliding, half running, he went down the hill toward the lonely farmhouse.

John Stevens and his mother were having one of their arguments. Or maybe, thought John angrily, it was just part of the same argument they'd had for the whole six months since his father's funeral. Whichever it was, he was sick and tired of it. Sick of being nagged at and tired of trying to explain that a man nearly eighteen years old didn't need his mother to tell him what to do.

"You don't understand!" he shouted at her. "You don't want to understand!"

She kept stirring the soup on the stove. "I don't know what's come over you," she said. "You were always such a good boy before your father died."

"Leave him out of this," he said hoarsely. (It was true, he had been different then, secure in his father's strength, not tortured and twisted by doubts, as now. But so had his mother been different.)

The change began in the moment that they turned from his father's grave and walked slowly through the thick June grass to the car the undertaker had provided. Even in his grief he had been proud of her that day, of her ash-blond prettiness accentuated by a black dress, of her self-control, of the way she said exactly the right thing to the friends and neighbors who came up shyly to say, "If there's anything I can do, Mrs. Stevens—"

"Thank you. I'll make free to call you if there is. Thank you."

He whispered to her consolingly, "I can work the farm. Don't worry, Mother."

"The farm? We're going to sell the farm," she said indifferently, flatly.

He was shocked. "But I *want* to be a farmer, you know I've always wanted to. Why on earth—"

"Not now. We'll talk about it later."

Later, however, never came. When he tried to reopen the subject, she was tired or had a headache, and if he persisted, she turned irritable. "I'm not up to discussing it, John. Can't you see that?"

Well, he couldn't. She hadn't wept—not one single tear—and, except that she didn't seem to want to talk to him, her behavior was as it had always been. Serene and cool, she went about her work, laying out clean clothes for him, having a hot meal waiting for him when he came in from the fields. "Aren't the roses doing well?" she'd say.

"I guess so, Mother." Their conversations never rose above this inconsequential level.

That first month he had been too absorbed in his sorrow to think. Everywhere he went, every day, there were so many reminders of his father: the corncrib, finished that very spring; the neat patching on Nellie's harness; the new gutter for the pump; worst of all, his father's old red sweater hanging on its nail just inside the barn door. John always touched the sweater gently as he went by, and it turned a little, revealing the darned sleeve and the sagging pocket where his father had carried his pipe. More than one evening, frustrated by his mother's silence, he went out to the barn to lean his face against the sweater and weep for all the warmth and cheer that his father had taken out of the world with him.

The second week of July, as he turned into the drive from a trip to town, he saw the Farm For Sale sign standing sturdily on the rim of the front lawn. He stared at it for a long time, unable to realize that his mother had so betrayed him.

She was sealing jelly glasses in the kitchen and she smiled nervously when he came in. "Well, how were things in town? Did Luther's have the right kind of paint?"

"You're selling the farm."

"I told you I was going to. We talked about it."

"No, we didn't. You're really selling?"

She kept on working, not looking at him. "Why, what else could I do? The land's worn out, the buildings are poor—"

"That's not true. The land is—"

"And you have four years of college to get through. Plenty of time for you to be a farmer after that."

"College," he said tonelessly. "I'm not going to college."

"Of course you are. Weren't you third highest in your class? Your father always planned to—"

"That was then. I can't do it now. Where would the money come from?"

"Why, from selling the farm. Where else?"

Like a mole uprooted by the plow and thrown into

strange, merciless light, he looked about him. This was Home. He loved it, could not imagine a life without it. He had supposed it would be here always, for him to come back to. Some of this feeling he tried to express to her, but his words were halting and inadequate and she cut him off with an amused look. "This old place? We'll be lucky to find somebody who'll take it off our hands."

In the face of such blasphemy he was speechless. His mother rattled on, moving briskly from table to stove. "I talked the whole thing over with Aunt Fay when she came up from Lansing for the funeral. She's all alone in that big house and she'll be glad to have us come live with her. We'll pay our share, of course, and it'll be a drop in the bucket compared to what you'd have to pay if you lived in a dormitory."

"Lansing?" he said stupidly. "Why are we going to live in Lansing?"

"Because Michigan State College is there, silly."

But that was not the real reason. He knew it by the way her eyes refused to meet his. All through supper he sat silent while she related the details of the plan that she had conceived and executed without a word to him. There'll be enough money to see you through, John, and a little left for my old age." The false, overly sweet smile that he had noticed earlier in the day reappeared. "I may even get myself a job as a saleslady somewhere, to help out. I'd enjoy that, I think."

For a week he slept badly, pondering the reasons behind her nervous haste to get away. The answer eluded him. Whenever he was with her he was quiet and watchful; and day and night he was racked by a terrible homesickness. He left his food almost untouched, but his mother did not notice. She had become a stranger. He no longer knew anything about her.

From the day the For Sale sign went up, he stopped trying to work the land. Instead, he found a job at a garage in town, riding back and forth on his bicycle morning and evening. Besides the independence it gave him, there was the swapping of stories with the men who hung around the garage, the staying in of an evening to go to a show or shoot a game of pool, the pedaling home at midnight with juke-box tunes humming through his head. No harm in any of it, and it lessened his misery a little.

His mother's objections were indirect. "Don't you want to come right home from work and review your trigonometry awhile tonight?" And once when she smelled beer on his breath she reproached not him but his new friends. "A wild, worthless lot, that crowd."

He answered defiantly, "I like them. You don't have to." He would not have admitted the savage delight he took in her perturbation.

The last word, naturally, had been hers. Late in September she showed him a check. "Option money. I believe the Michaelsons are going to buy it."

"It's—really sold then."

"I think so." She went over to the mirror above the fireplace. "I believe I'll go downtown tomorrow and buy a new hat." She leaned toward the glass, smiling a little. "I saw one in Forster's window that—You'll need some new clothes too, John."

Watching her touch her hair and turn her head, he realized again that she was an attractive woman, and instantly the answers he had been seeking came to him. Life in this quiet place, with only a son, wasn't enough for her. She had invented the flimsy excuse about his going to college because she needed stir and bustle and people, and she was going where she could find them. How bored she must have been, even while his father was alive, to be in such a hurry now! Perhaps she was dreaming already of a second and more satisfactory marriage. This, under the guise of self-sacrifice for her son's future! Her lack of honesty revolted him.

Disillusionment bitter in his mouth, he said carefully, "I'd like to ask you a favor. Will you give back the option money and sell the farm to me?"

"Why, how could—"

Rapidly, earnestly, he went on. "You'd have to wait awhile for your money, but you have Dad's insurance to tide you over. You go on to Aunt Fay's and I'll stay here and work at the garage until I have enough for a down payment. After that I'll farm the place and send you so much every month. You won't lose anything by it, I promise."

"Don't be ridiculous," she said crossly. "Leave you here, all by yourself? Who'd look after you?"

"I wouldn't be alone for long. In a year or two I'd get married, maybe, and—"

She laughed right in his face. "Hattie Monaghan, I suppose. And she's only sixteen."

Patiently he kept on. "She won't always be sixteen. 'Course it might not be Hattie. I haven't thought much about—"

"Oh, it'd be Hattie, all right, that shiftless father of hers is just waiting to palm her off on the first fellow that wants her. She's pretty and cute and she'll have six children by the time she's twenty-five, and you'll work your head off here in this backwoods all your life looking after the slew of them. No, I won't hear of it!"

"Don't talk to me as if I were a child!" he shouted. "I'm not a child!"

She turned her back on him, decisively, and there was a grim determination in her aspect that forbade another word. He might have been a four-year-old having a tantrum instead of a young man seeking a plan on which to reconstruct his life.

From then on he made a point of coming home only to sleep. Actually Hattie was not important to him, but as he lay on the garage floor staring at the underbellies of automobiles his thoughts came back to the girl again and again. She dominated his mind as a symbol of the independence he coveted. Married, he would be a man, not a possession of his mother's; and Hattie's warm breathlessness and soft laughter would fill the void that his mother's indifference to him had left. He made plans for an imaginary elopement. He tried to imagine what it would be like to live with the Monaghans until he had money enough to set up a separate place. Once he went so far as to call Hattie on the garage phone, but the line was busy and he did not try again.

Thus, wavering and indecisive, bristling with the fury of the helpless, he came to the day of departure. Bricker's grocery truck would come in a few hours to take him and his mother, bag and baggage, to the railroad station in town, and he was still quarreling, still trying to make a stand.

"I won't go with you," he said roughly. "I've told you a hundred times, I'm not going."

His mother tied an apron over her black suit. "I'll get us an early supper. There may not be a diner on the train."

"I don't want any supper."

"Then get out of here, with your sulking and scowling!" Her eyes were bright and hard. "And have the decency not to make me come calling you when the truck gets here."

He slammed the kitchen door behind him and walked out to the woodpile in front of the barn. He was, finally, defeated. She was not going to unbend, and inexperience made him shy away from complete rebellion. All he could do now was to hate her. He picked up the ax and began chopping furiously, the white chips leaping up to sting his face.

Wrapped in his misery, he did not hear the man approach. Suddenly, like an apparition, there he was, standing on the far side of the woodpile, watching. A tall, thin man, dressed in gray. A stranger.

"Hello, kid," said the man easily. "My name's Jack Norwood and I've got a truck with a flat tire down the road a ways. Can I use your phone?"

"We don't have a phone. The nearest one's two miles away, in town."

Norwood's black eyes darted around the barnyard. "No car either? Must be mighty peaceful around here. How do you stand it, a young guy full of beans, like you?"

"I'm used to it," John said briefly. He propped the ax against the wood. "I work at a garage. Maybe I can help out."

"Hell, no. I need a new tire. My spare went flat this morning."

"I've got a bike I could ride into town on. Somebody'd

17

come out from the garage." The moment he made the offer he wished he hadn't. He didn't like this man's face, nor the queer way he kept looking around. He added awkwardly, "Except I couldn't get back in time for a—sort of date I've got."

The man chewed his underlip. "Your dad around? Or a brother, maybe?"

"No. Just my mother and me." (He shouldn't have said that, he was handling this all wrong.)

"She in the house?"

"Yes, getting supper."

Norwood smiled and his manner became more authoritative. "Listen, I'm cold. Got an old coat or something I could borrow? Didn't expect to be stranded out on the road like this. I ain't dressed for it."

"Well, I don't know—"

Keeping his face toward John, the man made a quick, sidling semicircle toward the barn door. "How about this old red sweater? Just the ticket."

There was no time to object. Norwood was buttoning the sweater, nervy as you please. "I can find you something better than that," John said weakly. He hated seeing his father's sweater on this man, but he didn't know what to do about it.

"This'll do." The man smiled again, without mirth. "This'll do fine." He pulled the sweater well down and looked toward the house.

"My bike's right by the back door," John said hastily. "If you'd like to ride into town yourself—"

"Later, maybe. Let's go in the house a minute. I'd like to get warmed up."

"I don't think—"

"Come on!" He gave John a push that nearly knocked him down, still grinning to show it was all in fun. "Your mom might even shell out with a cup of coffee. If you asked her."

Here was the chance he'd been fighting his mother for —the right to take charge of what might be a serious situation—and he was flunking it simply because he didn't know how to go about making a stand. How could he be sure that the fellow was dangerous, instead of just ignorant? You couldn't knock a man down for borrowing an old sweater and asking for a cup of coffee! Reluctantly he led the way to the porch and noticed that Norwood had brought the ax along. The sight sent an added thrill of alarm along his nerves. He dared to say, "We usually leave the ax in the barn."

"Oh, thought I was helping you out. I'll just leave it inside the kitchen door."

Inside the kitchen door. Not outside. That cinched it. The man was now in complete authority and, willy-nilly, John was the Trojan horse, taking the enemy into the citadel.

By little signals, by putting all his anxiety in his eyes when Norwood wasn't looking, he tried to warn his mother to be on her guard. She didn't notice. Chatting placidly, she put another plate on the table, apologizing for the fact that their good dishes were already packed. Norwood ate supper with them, taking the seat nearest the door, where the ax stood. He spoke monosyllabically and John spoke not at all because of the schemes that raced through his mind. Remarks he could make that would lead Norwood to think they were not as cut off from assistance as they seemed. A way to get rid of the ax. The remembering of a forgotten errand that would excuse him from the table and give him a chance to go for help. All of these had shortcomings: either they left his mother at the mercy of the stranger or they might precipitate instant action on Norwood's part. No. Better to stall for time and hope for the best.

"You're not eating, John," said his mother.

"I'm not hungry."

"I'll see if I can find a jar of those peaches you like." She went into the pantry room and he could hear the rustle of paper as she searched among the jars, all ready in their cartons.

Norwood wiped his mouth and stood up decisively. "I've got to be going," he said. The humorless smirk came back to his face and he reached a long arm over to Mrs. Stevens' purse, lying on a chair. "Any money in here, I wonder?"

John forgot about the ax. The sight of those insolent fingers pawing through his mother's possessions made him angrier than he had ever been in his life before. "Put that down," he said ominously.

The man ignored him. "Ten dollars, for God's sake!" he said. "That's just like you dumb backwoods monkeys. Only ten bucks in the house!"

John leaped for him, but the man was quick. His left hand whipped out and caught the boy low in the stomach, doubling him up, with a paralyzing pain. "Don't try to fight in the big leagues, sonny. You're lucky I don't decide to wreck this whole place, just for the hell of it."

Gasping, John tried to straighten up. Then, through his giddiness, he heard his mother's voice. "Drop that purse and get out," she said.

Inexplicably, Norwood changed his tune. "Listen, lady," he whined, "this is all a big mistake. I didn't mean—"

The haze cleared and he saw now that his mother had a gun—his father's old shotgun, which they kept in the corner of the pantry. She must have forgotten that it wasn't loaded. "Get out of here!" she said, and he saw her finger whiten on the futile trigger.

Norwood saw it too and backed away. "Don't get excited, lady. I'm goin'." But his hand was groping behind him for the ax. John saw it just in time.

"No, you don't!" he yelled, and snatched the ax away from the seeking fingers, lifted it above his head for the stroke that would lay the enemy at his feet.

The man didn't wait. He was out the door like a scalded cat, grabbing the bicycle as he passed it, running with it down the drive until he reached the road, where he vaulted into the seat and disappeared around the curve.

Taking deep, triumphant breaths of the cold air that poured through the kitchen, John watched him go. The sensation of miserable helplessness was gone. Instead, he felt light, wonderful, shaken with inward laughter at the sight of a man running away from *him*! Closing the door, he disdained to lock it. "If he tries to come back, I'll settle his hash for *sure*!" he said, and meant it.

The new confidence that had come to him had missed his mother. She was leaning against the sink, the gun drooping in her hands, her face alarmingly white. Gently he took the gun from her and led her to a chair. "It's all right now, Mother. It's all over. Here, I'll get you some coffee."

In the moment of crisis, she had seemed to fill the room, but he saw now how little actual strength she had. She was all spirit, and his heart swelled with love and admiration for her. He put an arm around her shoulders and held the cup to her lips for the first few swallows. "You drink the rest of that and you'll be all right." He straddled the kitchen chair across from her and smiled reassuringly whenever her pitifully blank eyes looked at him.

"The gun wasn't loaded," she said vaguely.

"I knew, but I didn't think you did." He took one of her cold trembling hands and chafed it. His voice was respectful. "That took a lot of nerve. You're a real, honest-to-God heroine."

Her face crumpled into weeping. "I'm not. I'm not at all. You don't know how it's been—" The great gasping sobs would not let her speak. She put her head down on the table and cried as if she would never stop.

He waited until the worst of it was over. Then he brought cold water and sponged her face with it, talking softly the whole time. "We have to get you in shape," he said. "Bricker'll be along to pick us up in less than an hour. We'll stop off at the police station to tell them about Norwood, and then we'll go to the depot. You can't get on a train looking like this."

"I'm not going to get on the train," she said wildly. "It's too much, to lose everything at once! First your father, and then my house—oh, I knew what was sensible and I tried, but I can't, I can't. Not even for you!"

"Yes, you can. Come on, now. Pull yourself together." He knelt beside her and raised her swollen face. "I know how you feel, and it won't do. There's no sense living in the past. You were right and I was wrong. We've got to go ahead. Just the way you planned."

She looked at him then, and saw him. "I'm sorry. I—it was your father's sweater and the funny look on your face—and when he hit you, I wanted to kill him!"

"It's all over. Don't think about it any more."

"All right. I'll try." She wiped her eyes and smiled shakily. "I'm all in pieces. No good to you at all. I can't even think what's still to be done."

He began picking up the dishes, briskly. "Never mind," he said. "I'll take care of everything. Count on me."

"Anything else, Ella?" asked Mr. Sims, stuffing the groceries into a big brown bag. "Here's a little pack of candies I'm throwing in for the kids. Wouldn't hurt you to have a few, either."

Ella Mack smiled shyly at him. Mr. Sims had always been kind to her, from the days when her eyes barely came above the level of the counter. She had been a plain, undernourished child, beset by the care of younger half brothers, anxious over the health of a frail, weak mother, terrified of her rough, loudmouthed stepfather; and Mr. Sims had made her feel important, somehow, and valuable and pretty. He still made her feel that way, now that she was a plain and unattractive twenty.

"I'll call Jimmy to carry these out to the car for you, Ella."

The customary terror in which she lived rushed back,

expunging the little interval of warmth and safety. Jimmy Blake had gone to high school with her, and she would be expected to talk to him: a few words about the weather, or the condition of her family's old black Ford, or the doings of people whom they both knew. She was not equal to it, her timidity forbade it. "I'll carry them myself, Mr. Sims. I'm used to lifting things."

He helped her himself then, fussing a little about her driving the five miles home without a heater in the car. "Seems like your family ought to care a little more about you," he said, "seeing as how you do all the work for them. If you don't insist on your own rights, Ella, nobody will."

"I guess I'm not much of an insister, Mr. Sims."

Pulling away from the curb, she felt gay and a little reckless. Though she dare not be more than five minutes late getting home, she risked making a little circle of the town, seeing all the lights come on through the dusk. The State Police Post, next to the bank. The movie house, where she had never been allowed to go. Elnicky's Bar, her stepfather's hangout. The high school. The little house where Miss Lewis lived and where Ella might have lived too, if everything had been different.

Thinking of Miss Lewis always made her feel good, and she was smiling as she left the town behind her and headed out on the state road. Miss Lewis was the school district's nurse, with her office in the high school, where Ella had first met her. That day Miss Lewis had been rushed off her feet giving eye and teeth examinations to four hundred incoming freshmen, and she had picked on Ella for help, at random.

"You, girl. What's your name? Well, Ella, I need a hand

here. Keep these fresh packages coming, and jot down what I tell you to on these cards. All right, Jim, sit down here and let's have a look at you. Last time I saw you, you were seven and had the measles. What's the idea of coming in here all grown up and making me feel old?"

Ella had helped Miss Lewis all that morning, shoulder to shoulder, as if they were equals. Miss Lewis didn't give a lot of directions and fuss at you; she gave you a job, took it for granted that you had the sense to do it, and turned her attention to her own work. At noon she threw herself into a chair and looked up at Ella.

"You're good," she said. "The principal usually assigns me a girl for an assistant. Couple of hours' work every day, pays a dollar an hour. How'd you like to be the girl this year?"

It was the first time in her life that Ella had been asked to make a decision of her own, and she made it quickly. "I'd like to, Miss Lewis."

"I'll fix it up then. You realize it'll mean you'll have no study periods. You'll have to do all your studying at home."

"I can do that."

She did, too, though she suffered for it. Her stepfather, Gus, jawed at her every day. "A big girl, fourteen, settin' around with her face in a book when she ought to be helping her maw! Let me tell you, Miss High-and-Mighty, you're not going to get at them books till you've done every last thing that needs to be done in this house!"

Her mother, half ill from yearly birthing or miscarriage, tried to stand up for her. "Ella does more than she ought to, as it is. She has a right to an education."

"What's a woman need education for? All these laws

25

about kids having to go to school till they're sixteen! Poppycock!"

The thing that saved her was the ten dollars she brought home each week. Gus came to count on it. She handed it to him each Friday evening and he would be off to El-nicky's, stumbling home any time after midnight. It was worth the price to her, to have the long evening alone with her mother and the kids, all of them free from Gus's bruising tyranny. They became quite gay, those evenings. The children popped corn, laughing and chattering, and Ella and her mother set each other's hair and looked through the mail-order catalogue at the new styles. When Gus complained during the week of not feeling well, they lived on pins and needles lest he be not well enough to go out Friday night. Fortunately Gus was always well enough for that.

She said nothing about her home to Miss Lewis, ever, but somehow Miss Lewis came to know. At the beginning of Ella's junior year Miss Lewis said, "It's not right that you can't have a pretty dress or two and some new shoes. How do you expect to go to the class parties? You earn the money, you're entitled to spend some of it."

"I wouldn't be allowed to go to any parties anyway. My goodness!"

Miss Lewis looked thoughtful. "Would it help if I went out and talked to him, Ella?"

"No, oh no. It would make it worse."

"Is he going to let you graduate?"

"Yes, I think so."

The nurse's eyes twinkled behind her glasses. "I rather thought he might, considering those ten dollars a week.

What are you going to do after you're through school?"

"Nothing," she said bleakly. "I'll just be home all the time then. Gus doesn't believe in women working—outside the house, that is. He doesn't mind how hard they work there."

"He seems to like a little extra money coming in. Where will be get it?"

"The boys'll be old enough to have jobs then. Paper routes or working in a store. He'll have their money."

"You'll be eighteen next year, Ella. Your own boss. You can do whatever you want to then."

"There's nothing I want to do, really, except go to college, and that's out of the question."

"St. Luke's Hospital isn't out of the question." Miss Lewis sat forward on her chair, starch rustling. "Now listen. You're intelligent and conscientious, and you have a real ability for nursing. If I recommend you to St. Luke's, they'll take you into training and it won't cost you a cent. It's a hard profession, nursing, but a good one. How about it?"

Ella closed her eyes on the marvelous vision and swallowed. "I couldn't. I'd love to, but he'd never let me."

The nurse looked exasperated. "You're not even his own child! He has five of his own. Let them help out. You've done your share."

There was no way of telling Miss Lewis how Gus really was. The rages. The oaths. The blows. "I'm sorry, Miss Lewis. It's wonderful of you, but I—couldn't."

"You're afraid of him," said Miss Lewis simply.

"I guess so. You don't know how awful he can be."

"You'd be away from home. He couldn't get at you."

"He'd take it out on the rest of them. I'd—worry so that it wouldn't be worth it."

"But your mother picked him out. It's up to her to cope with him. All you have to do is tell him you're going to be a nurse, and if he raises Cain, face him down! Stand up to him!"

Hopeless as urging jelly to turn into brick! Ella had not dared mention St. Luke's even to her mother, who might precipitate calamity by broaching the subject to her husband. There had been nothing to do, after commencement, but fall into the hurried back-breaking routine of the unhired help in an overpopulated household. It was the price she was willing to pay for peace, the toll exacted by Gus's violence. Even now, driving the rattletrap car through the early dark, she was anxious about how things might be going at home. Guiltily, because she had loitered, she pressed harder on the accelerator.

She saw the obstacle in the road just in time. Her brakes cried out, the wheels sent up sprays of gravel, the motor coughed and stalled. She peered over the steering wheel at the object her headlights had picked up. A bicycle, lying in the middle of the road! Her eyes searched the road margins for a sprawled child, but she saw no one. Gingerly she stepped out in the road, raised the bicycle, looked for bloodstains. So intent was she that when a hand touched her arm she screamed and heard the high, wailing echo calling back from the woods.

"That's enough of that, sweetheart!" the man said. He clapped a rough hand over her mouth and talked close to her ear. "You're going to drive me across the state line to Wentworth. Shut up and get in the car. I haven't any time to waste."

Holding her by the arms, he thrust her into the driver's seat and swore when he looked at the gas gauge. "Damn it, there isn't enough in here to go sixty miles!"

"The gauge doesn't work," she said stupidly.

"Well, let's get going. If we have to stop anywhere, I'm your uncle Jack and don't forget it." He pressed her arm, numbingly. "Get it?"

"Yes."

She started the engine and, once they were under way, he seemed to relax a little. "I bet I came twenty miles on that stinking contraption. Feels good to sit down. You live around here?"

"Yes."

"Not gabby, are you? Well, that's all right with me." He took a heavy monkey wrench out from under his sweater. "See this? I'm going to take a little nap, and if you try any funny business—"

She did not hear all of what he said. She was conscious of a difficulty in breathing and the heavy thudding of her heart, but otherwise her mind was blank. She drove automatically, sitting as far from him as she could. Not until she heard a snore did she dare to look at him. There he sat, horrible even in sleep, slack mouth open, the wrench tightly in his hand. A nightmare that had escaped from dreams into reality. Terrifying. Impossible. Yet there he was.

For half an hour she drove by mere reflex action, and then she discovered a truth: fear, when it is extreme, does not last. Her mind threw off the inertia of shock and gave her a glimmer of hope. She was coming to the main highway on which she must turn to get to Wentworth, and there was a stop light or two there, a group of stores, some houses. There, surely, she could attract someone's attention—by making faces or signaling or dropping something out of the window. Or she might drive the car into something and take her chances in the wreck.

But the man awoke, sharply. "What're we coming to?"

"The main road into Wentworth. I'll turn left at that light."

"No. Go straight through."

"That'll take us to—"

"We'll find a back road into Wentworth."

The car bumped up to the smooth pavement, passed through the green halo of light, bumped down again to the gravel surface on the other side. "Good," he said with satisfaction. "Just do what I tell you and you'll be okay. I'm not a bad guy when you get to know me." He patted her knee approvingly.

"Why don't *you* drive?" she said desperately.

He pushed over closer to her and she felt his breath on her cheek. "Because I have to be sure you stay with me, sweetie. Can't have you running to the cops. And it ain't as easy for a driver to leave a car as it is for a passenger. See?"

"I won't go to the cops. Please. If you let me out right here, I'll let you take the car and I won't say a word. Honestly I—"

He buried his face in her neck and laughed. " 'Course

30

you won't. You're not going to get the chance. That's why."

"But after I drop you off at Wentworth, what's to stop me from going to the police then? You'll have to believe me sometime. You'll have to take my word for it. I won't tell the police, if only you'll—"

He paid no attention. He was pawing at her, babbling foolishly, and suddenly she grasped the significance of what he had half admitted. He could not risk turning her loose, no matter how she begged or promised. After she had served his various purposes he would kill her. Kidnapping, crossing a state line, criminal assault maybe, what did he have to lose? Her death was a necessity to him. Poor stupid little fool to take so long to realize that!

Since her death was inevitable and it no longer mattered what she did, she drove an elbow forcefully into his ribs. "Sit up and give me room! I can't drive like this."

He gave her space, leering. "You're right. Mustn't mix business with pleasure. Later we'll pull over somewhere and get friendly. What d'you say?"

She didn't answer. She was surveying her life with detachment, as if it were already over. To be dead in a ditch at twenty before she had even begun to live! Her revulsion was so great that she cranked down a window swiftly, to keep from being ill.

The man saw the headlights behind them before she did. "Somebody's following us," he said. "Turn down here and keep going." He sat tensely for five minutes, watching the back window. "Yep. They've turned after us, and they're coming fast. Hell!" He crouched down, gnawing excitedly at a fingernail. "Just over the next rise, turn off the lights and drive off the road into a field. Hurry!"

As they dropped down the next hill and she snapped off the lights obediently, he reached over and gave the wheel a mighty wrench. The car skidded, turned, leaped a culvert, and shuddered along over the rough ground where corn had been. Behind some tall shocks, he cut the motor and took the keys. In the stillness she heard the other car pass by, following the road.

"Do you know where we are?" he asked fiercely. "Have any idea?"

"No."

"I'm going to take a quick look around. They might be bluffing, themselves." He got out, dropping the keys into his pocket. "Stay here if you know what's good for you. I won't be far away. If I have to run after you and bring you back—" He lingered a second, and she knew that he was debating whether it would be safer to destroy her now. But she was a woman and he had another use for her, when he got around to it. A man he would have killed on the spot.

He moved away and she lost sight of him immediately in the thick darkness. Her hand crept to the door handle, and she waited. A sixth sense must have warned her that the time was not yet, because she did not hear him return until he was right beside her. "Just checking up," he said threateningly, and went away again.

This time she didn't wait. She pressed the handle softly and was free, running across the field, dodging behind the corn shocks, going away from the road toward the farmhouse that must be somewhere ahead. He was after her, almost from the start. She heard him swear and stumble, and once, when he circled ahead to cut her off, she almost ran into him. She threw herself on the ground and he passed within a yard of her without knowing it.

She never knew when he got into the car and drove away. It may have been during one of the periods when she was having a vomiting attack, pressing her face against a corn shock to stifle the sound of retching. Between the nausea and the listening, it took her an hour to reach the lighted space near a barn where a man in overalls was working on a tractor motor. "May I use your telephone?" she said to him, and fell on her knees from sheer inability to stand any longer.

Their name was Benson, and they were very kind. Mr. Benson did the telephoning, first to the state police and then to Ella's mother. "No, she's all right, ma'am. The police are coming out to talk to her and they'll drive her home. She's been a mighty brave girl, I'd say. Mighty brave." Mrs. Benson fed her a lavish supper and sponged her stained coat into respectability, marveling, "My goodness, I don't know how you lived through it! I wouldn't have had the nerve!"

"It isn't hard to have the nerve when you know you're going to be killed anyway." A thought struck her and she paused, her fork halfway to her mouth. "But—you always *are* going to die anyway, aren't you?" she said slowly. "Eventually, I mean."

"Well, everybody dies, if that's what you're talking about," said Mrs. Benson, puzzled. " 'But as for man, his days are as the grass,' you know." She smiled consolingly. "You're young. You have a long time ahead of you, never fear."

The police were kind too. Lieutenant Harris said that her mother was probably anxious to see her and they'd better do their talking while they drove. So at sixty miles an hour she answered a hundred questions, and Sergeant Connors, in the back seat, jotted down the answers. Finally she put a question of her own: "Who was he?"

"His name's Jake Norris. Escaped from the Prison Farm this afternoon. Supposed to be doing ten years at hard labor. He's a bad customer, miss. You're lucky."

"I think he was going to kill me."

"Murder, robbery, rape, he's done 'em all. The only conviction we could make stick in this state was assault with intent to kill. We sent him up for that." He turned his head slightly and spoke to the sergeant. "If he's heading for Wentworth, he must mean to catch a train to Chicago."

"Could be. That's his old stamping ground, the files said."

"We'll have to head him off. Once he's in Chicago, he'll be mighty hard to find."

They let her off by the walk that led to the porch, and her mother came running down the steps, reaching out grateful arms to her. "Thank God, Ella. I've been so worried. Are you really all right? You aren't hurt?"

"I'm fine, Mom."

"Your father's kinda upset. You know how he gets. Don't pay any attention to what he says. He—"

"You'll catch cold," Ella said calmly. "Let's go in."

The children were waiting for her just inside the door, and she hugged them, smiling to show that she was unharmed. Then she walked across the room to where Gus stood, red-faced and glowering.

"I'm sorry about your car," she said. "The police think they'll get it back for you."

"Stoppin' to pick up strangers!" he bellowed. "After all you've been told! I ought to—"

"Oh, keep quiet a minute," she said impatiently.

Gus's jaw dropped. In the sudden stillness she heard her mother gasp, saw the grin on her oldest brother's face. The resolution that had been forming in her mind crystallized, rock-hard.

"I'm leaving here tonight," she told him. "I'm going in to stay with Miss Lewis for a few days. Until she can get me into the Nurses' Training School at St. Luke's. I'm going to learn to be a nurse."

Gus recovered and started for her, hand upraised. "I'll learn you to talk to me like that, you little snip! I'll—"

She did not retreat a step. A bright mounting anger threw color into her cheeks and brought a glint into her eye that her stepfather didn't relish. "You lay a hand on me, Gus, and it'll be the sorriest day of your life! I mean it!"

He dropped the hand and tried to cover bafflement with bluster. "Talkin' big won't get you noplace. You keep it up and I'll take a belt to you! I'm warnin' you—"

"No, I'm warning *you*. The next time I hear of you beating one of these kids I'm going to report you to the county authorities. You're not a fit person to have charge of children and everybody knows it! It's high time something was done about it."

Her mother whispered fearfully, "Ella, Ella, don't."

"There's nothing to be afraid of, Mom. They have laws for people like him." She turned her back deliberately on the strangled sounds which were all that Gus's loose mouth could utter. "I guess they pay me a little money, even while I'm learning. I'll send it to you."

"No, honey. You keep it for yourself. I—this is all so quick that I—won't you even take off your coat?"

"The bus is nearly due." She hugged her mother and reached out a hand to the youngsters. "I'll write. Every week. And after I graduate I'll have a house and you can all come and stay with me whenever you like. I'll miss you so much."

They clustered around her, talking and weeping, and her mother said, "I'm glad for you, you know that. But to go tonight—right after that awful man worried us so—"

"I'm two years late now, Mom. The sooner the better."

Gus had decided to change his tune. The kid really meant to go, and she was a lot of help around the place. He advanced with a forgiving air. "Maybe I was a little hasty, Ella. Seems like we ought to talk this over, reach an understanding. I'm a reasonable man—"

She laughed. She couldn't help it. "I've had a good many years of your reasonableness. I don't want another minute of it."

He clutched a chair back, his knuckles whitening. "I've heard all I want to hear from you. Now you get out of here. This minute. Don't wait to pack your clothes."

"What clothes?" she said, walking toward the door.

They all followed her, and her oldest brother said, "It's pretty dark, Sis. Want me to walk you to the bus?"

"Thanks, Jerry, but you'd better stay here with Mom. I'm not afraid."

It was wonderful to know as she walked down the lane, turning to wave at them through her tears, that she would never be afraid of anything again.

People said that the only reason old Walt Sparks didn't live in a shack, in spite of all his money, was that he was sentimental about the big house. He had lived there always; first with his mother, who had died when Walt was forty; for the next ten years with his wife and baby son; and from then on by himself, and he was now in his seventieth year. A long time to live in one house.

Among his neighbors in the widely scattered houses around the lake, to the tradespeople in Wentworth, twenty miles away, old Walt was known as a recluse, a hermit. "The old boy's getting queerer every day," they said. "It's a wonder young Doc Sparks doesn't keep more of an eye on his dad." The older, wiser heads guessed that young Doc Sparks had tried and that his father had resisted. "Old Walt doesn't want to have anything to do with anybody," they said. "Afraid it might cost him money. He's still got the first dime he ever earned. Wonder what he's going to do with it?"

Still, if the old gentleman had no ultimate plans, he did have a way of life. Each Friday he drove into Wentworth to collect his rents, visit his bank, pick up his meager supplies. Much as he deplored the expense of a car, it was necessary that he have one, for this. Six days a week it sat in the garage; but on the seventh, rain or shine, he wheeled it slowly out and made his way to town. Years ago he had bought inexpensive cars, but he had found that they didn't hold up the way they should. Now he owned a big black Lincoln, powerful and certain, five years old and apparently impervious to wear. He did not consider it an extravagance, he could justify its cost to himself.

It was a little harder to justify his gun collection. Sometimes, taking the pistols, the rifles, the muskets down from their racks, fingering the smooth metal, oiling and reloading carefully, he felt a qualm through his pleasure. One gun, for protection, yes. But twenty-five guns? On these occasions he reminded himself hastily that every man had a right to one foible, that, since he lived frugally, without a telephone, without automatic heat or hot water, without new clothes or the gadgets that were necessities to other people, he had a right to a comparatively inexpensive weakness. The sight of the loaded guns lying quiescent in their racks gave him a feeling of power, of self-sufficiency, that was very warming. He had never fired a gun in his life.

His most genuine passion, however, was the house. It had fourteen rooms, all high-ceilinged, many with fireplaces, which were useful, because heat crept slowly through the lower floor and reached the upper ones not at all. The wood-burning stove in the kitchen kept him warm while he prepared his meals, and he usually went to bed early, rolling himself into the old-fashioned quilts and bulky comforters. Stove, fireplace brass, and bedding he kept immaculate. He tended the house as carefully as his mother had, polishing, sweeping, dusting, airing. Each day he lowered the window shades against the sun, and twice a year he tugged the big carpets outside, hung them on a line, beat them vigorously. All the rooms were kept open and livable, mahogany glowing, antimacassars primly placed on the chair backs though no heads ever rested against them. His son's wife Isabelle sniffed at all this, had said something once about false gods and idolatry. "This isn't a house, it's a shrine," she had said disturbingly.

He answered crossly, "That's foolish. A shrine for what?"

"I don't know, Father Sparks. I thought maybe you did."

He didn't care for Isabelle, couldn't imagine why George had married her. One of those smarty Eastern-school girls who talked right up to a man. She didn't come out any more with George on his weekly visits. Said she had to stay with the children, and he was just as glad. Matter of fact he'd said more than once that he'd just as soon George didn't come out either.

"Seems to me a young doctor, getting started, would have something better to do with his time," he told George.

"I don't like to think of you all alone out here without a soul near in case something happened to you. I just come to check up."

"Well, you don't have to. There's nothing the matter with me."

George looked amused. "I won't muss up the place,

Dad. Ten minutes, once a week. You can put up with that."

"All foolishness!"

"I don't know that it is. With your asthma and blood pressure—"

"You don't know a thing about my blood pressure! I don't hold with doctors. Never did."

"Well, put it that I worry about you."

He would have liked to say, "Worry about my money, most likely!" but he knew that wasn't true. George didn't have sense enough to care about money. Not practical. Namby-pamby and soft, the way May had been.

Old Walt's mother had warned him against marrying May. "She's not our kind, Walter. She'll never make a good, careful, hard-working wife." But within a year of his mother's death he had married the smiling, prettily complexioned creature, and for a while all had been beer and skittles. They had romped through the house like a couple of kids, treated themselves to trips and movies, and sat down every night to May's beautiful and extravagant dinners. He was as charmed as a man from the dim, frozen Arctic suddenly let loose in a tropical island paradise.

Occasionally, looking over the grocery bill, he felt a pang. "Two pounds of butter in one week. May!"

"Well, I baked that Scotch shortbread you liked, and—"

"But two pounds!"

She put her soft arms around his neck. "We can afford it, Walter, can't we?"

At first he said that they could. As the years after George's birth went by, however, his conscience troubled him increasingly. He had to admit that May asked very

40

little for herself, but she was insatiable in demanding things for the child. They began to quarrel about whether a new furnace should be put in, and the price of vitamin tablets, and how fast George outgrew his shoes and if he should be allowed to play in the living room.

"I tell you, May, he's wearing out the furniture! Climbing all over it and nicking pieces out of the legs with those fool toys of his."

"He doesn't climb over it. It's just that his legs aren't long enough to sit in it properly, and his heels—"

"I don't care what it is! You keep him off that furniture!"

"Do you really expect the furniture to last forever, Walter? Do you honestly believe you'll never have to buy another stick till the day you die? Isn't furniture supposed to be used and wear out?"

"Not if it's properly taken care of," he said stubbornly.

"I do take care of it. But if my son isn't allowed to sit on a chair, or eat his meals at the table—"

"God knows he eats! Meat every day."

"The doctor says he needs it. He says everyone—"

"Don't mention the doctor to me. Of all the silly waste! You'd think a kid couldn't grow up by himself. In the old days—"

"In the old days a lot of them *didn't* grow up."

Once, in the midst of an argument, she said soberly, "Are you keeping something from me, Walter? Have we lost a lot of money? Are we poor?"

"We aren't yet, but we will be if you keep this up!"

Gradually she changed, became quieter, more conservative. The arguments ceased, and he was pleased at the improvement in her. Sometimes, coming into the house, he would hear her talking and laughing with the youngster, but when she heard his step she became silent and subdued. Evenings, after George was put to bed, she sat and sewed. She was an expert needlewoman and he enjoyed watching her at it.

"You look pretty doing that," he told her gruffly.

Her smile had a peculiar quality. "A good thing. I haven't bought a new dress in five years."

"Well, you don't need clothes. We don't go anywhere."

"No," she said agreeably, "and of course we don't have anyone in."

The grocery bills had long since become reasonable. She fed George separately and, though he had an idea that George got butter and lamb chops, he was pleased to see beans and potatoes and margarine on his own plate.

"Nobody could want a better meal than that," he said defiantly, wiping his lips.

She had taken to having only toast and tea for her dinner. "I'm glad you like it," she said politely.

When George was eight years old and in school all day, she suggested that she go back to her old job as a stenographer in Wentworth. "I believe they'd take me, even part time," she said. "I was good at it."

Much as the idea of the extra money appealed to him, he vetoed this. Certain things simply were not fitting, and a wife working outside her home was one of them. Especially a wife as frail-looking as May had become in the past few years. (Oh, these silly dieting fads that women took up!) He put his foot down and no more was said about the matter. Lulled by her outward meekness, he did not see that the storm signals were flying now in earnest.

George's tenth birthday arrived. Walt had been away on a business trip and he arrived home a day early, not to honor the occasion, for no one had reminded him of it, but quite by accident. He was amazed to find the house in a clatter with six boys running around in it, a birthday supper on the table, and a magnificent sheep-lined jacket, size 14, peeping from an open box. Fuming and fretting, he contained himself until they were alone. Then he waved the jacket in her face.

"What's this for, a young king? How much did you spend for this?"

"Eighteen dollars," she said crisply. "He needs it. It'll wear for two years at least."

He lost his temper completely. Pacing up and down amidst the wreckage of the birthday party, he spoke loudly and at length, ending up with the question he asked so often. "You'll ruin me! Do you think I'm a rich man?"

This time the query didn't shatter her. "Yes," she said angrily, "I do." Other words came flooding from her lips, her voice harsh with the freight of them. She gave him every figure: the value of each of his properties; the amount of rent he collected; the size of his savings and government bondholdings. "You're worth three hundred thousand dollars, and we live like paupers! I wouldn't mind, but we *aren't* poor and I'm sick of living as if we were. I saved the money for the party, it didn't cost you a cent. I shouldn't have had to do that. I should have a reasonable household allowance to manage. Every cent I have to ask you for, you make me feel like a criminal! Why should I have to crawl to you for the most ordinary little necessities!"

He said, with what dignity he could muster, "I'm putting by for the future. You'll be glad of it someday."

"I won't be glad of it. How much do we need for a future? We have enough right now for the rest of our lives. You'll keep right on scrimping to the edge of your grave, and what for?"

"There might come a time when we'll need it. Waste not, want not, my mother always said."

"Your mother was a poor girl from the Old Country. It's natural that, when she finally got a house and a nest egg, she'd hang onto them. But *you've* no excuse. You think you're saving for something, but you're not. You're saving because you enjoy it, because you think more of houses and furniture and money than you do of people!"

"Just because I won't let you be wasteful—"

She leaned toward him, her hands crushing the gaudy birthday trimmings on the table. "Answer me one thing, Walter. Will you send George to college when he's ready to go?"

"That's a long time off, May. Time to think about that when—"

"Right *now*. I want your promise. In writing. I want a legal contract with you that you'll send George to college."

"Maybe he won't want to go. After he finishes high school, perhaps he'll go into business or—"

"Would you help him get started in a business, then? Business or college, do you have any intention of doing something for him?"

He looked judicious. "Well now, that depends. Too much help makes a young fellow soft. I don't want him spoiled. He'll be all the better for coming up the hard way. You're being unreasonable, May."

She studied his face for a minute. Then, without another word, she began clearing the table. When she picked up the boy's new jacket to carry it upstairs, he said magnanimously, "He can keep that, since you've bought it. If he only wears it for good, it'll last a long time."

"Yes, he'll keep it," she said, and walked out of the room.

By the time he came home the next afternoon she had gone, taking the boy and every stitch that belonged to the two of them. He was too proud, too outraged, to go after them. And, with the first shock over, he had been glad to be alone again in the spotless, unlittered rooms, with no outward drains on his patience or his purse.

There had never been a divorce. May and George settled in Wentworth, and once in a while he saw her on Main Street there, hurrying to work. His lawyer advised him that the courts might allow her something for the child's maintenance, but she did not ask for anything and he did not offer it. She died when George was in medical school, and he allowed her to be buried in his family plot, though he did not attend the funeral. After all, they had not spoken to each other in thirteen years.

It was early in their separation, however, that he had made his will, to punish her. He had a second cousin, Agatha Munn, a sensible woman about his own age, widowed, making her living in Flint by running a very clean boardinghouse, where she set a plain but nourishing table. In Agatha's eyes Walt was a great man. On his rare visits she treated him with flattering deference, not only asking his advice on business matters but taking it. The two of them agreed on everything: that free milk for impoverished school children was a waste of taxpayers' money, since it further encouraged their parents in shiftless ways; that no one appreciated anything he got for nothing; that the amount of money a man acquired was an absolute measure of his intelligence.

It was to Agatha that he willed his fortune and his house. She would handle his affairs well, and she had a son as careful as herself to carry on after her. To May and George he put down a grudging thousand dollars apiece; and even after May's death he kept the will sturdily intact. He would teach the son the lesson that the mother hadn't had a chance to learn.

He swerved from this severity just once. On the occasion of George's graduation from medical school old Walt sent his son a check for fifty dollars. He regretted the impulse almost immediately, told himself that he had started something, that the boy would be expecting future handouts. And he was dumfounded when, on the very day that George moved into his combined house and office in Wentworth, he brought the check, still uncashed, out to the house.

"I don't need this, Dad. Thanks a lot, anyway."

Old Walt covered his relief by being gruff. "Didn't know you'd gotten so rich. Working your way through school must be more profitable than I thought."

"No, it isn't profitable. But you need this worse than I do."

Indignation made him reckless. "That's foolish! Do you have any idea how much I'm worth?"

"What you're worth to *whom*?" George said, smiling.

He couldn't figure out why he had felt insulted, nor why George, before he left, had seemed sorry about the whole thing. "Get this straight, Dad. I don't want your money. I'll never touch a cent of it. Let's forget all about how rich or poor we are and see if we can't build up some kind of relationship on that basis."

Crazy talk. Unbelievable. Yet, as the years hurried by and George faithfully kept up his visits, old Walt was forced to believe it. Test and probe as he might, he could not find a flaw in George's indifference to his wealth. The nearest he came was when George mentioned how badly Wentworth needed a hospital.

"Even a clinic would do. Three or four beds for emergency cases. Operating facilities. Every year we lose some patients who can't last out the trip to Meyersville. The town says they can't afford it. My opinion is they can't afford *not* to afford it."

Old Walt watched him from beneath his brows. "Might be a good thing for an old codger like me to sink my money into. Do some good before I go."

He saw the quick light on George's face, but it lasted only an instant. Then George laughed a little. "No, Dad. I wasn't hinting. You mustn't think of such a thing."

"Why mustn't I?" he said petulantly. "I didn't say I *would*, but what's so funny in my thinking about it?"

"Believe me, I was laughing at myself," George said apologetically.

He ignored this. "You treat me as if I were a kid, still

wet behind the ears. Got a swelled head, that's what's wrong with you. I'll think and do as I please!"

"What I meant was—well, if something I said made you decide to give Wentworth a clinic, look what would happen. You'd be unhappy the minute you'd done it. You'd feel bamboozled, and you'd be sorry, and you'd hold it all against *me*. That's the way you are and you can't help it. I don't want that kind of thing to happen. I want us to be —friends."

There was a pressure in the old man's chest and the faint, alarming pain he had noticed lately, but he managed to snarl, "Why should we be friends? What have I ever done for you? You come tramping in here without a bit of encouragement, and you belittle me to my face and probably laugh at me behind my back—"

"That's not so," said George reasonably. "I've never belittled or laughed either. And if you've never done anything for me, at least you've not done anything against me. According to your lights, you're honest and fair and, God knows, you're self-sufficient. I can admire you for those things, and I do. As to why I come here, isn't blood supposed to be thicker than water? I even think that you'd miss me a little if I didn't come, though I don't expect you to give me the satisfaction of saying so."

"Wouldn't miss you at all," muttered old Walt perversely.

To himself, he had to admit that George's visits made life more interesting. They talked about George's cases and the best spray for fruit trees and the proper kind of power mower to buy. He even enjoyed George's attempts at bossing him, though he opposed them stubbornly. He refused to have a telephone installed, he continued to change his own tires, shovel snow, prune the orchard, and paint the house. He snickered at any mention of balanced diet or vitamins. It so amused him to defy George on these matters that he arranged, each Friday evening, some remark that would outrage his son afresh.

"Went up on the roof and cleaned the gutters today," he would announce innocently. And George was off, talking warmly about the avoidance of strain on seventy-year-old hearts and the months in bed a broken hipbone would entail, while old Walt smiled wickedly to himself, the center of attention.

On this particular Friday evening, he came in at dusk from raking ancient leaves, knowing that George would see the great piles as he drove up and be ready with a lecture by the time he set foot inside the door. He puttered around the kitchen, frying ham and potatoes, making coffee; and after the last pan had been scoured he went to his desk by the fireplace in the living room, threw more hickory logs into the blaze, sighed heavily as he sat down. He was tired tonight, and there was no telling how late George would be. It depended on the number of calls the boy had to make. Once it had been eleven o'clock before he arrived, and old Walt had been asleep in a chair.

"This is too late for an early-rising gent like you to be up," George had said, "but I need a cup of coffee. I'm glad you waited."

"Wasn't waiting," he had answered gruffly. "Just happened to fall asleep down here, that's all."

Tonight he decided to occupy himself with checking the rent receipts and making up the cash on hand into tidy parcels to be locked away in his strongbox until his next visit to town. From one drawer he took his old leather money pouch, dropping it on the desk top with a solid, jingling thud. From another he brought out his account book.

As he lifted this, his eye was caught by the long white envelope that lay beneath. His last will and testament. A hundred times he had seen it there without disturbing it, but this time he picked it up and sat turning the envelope in his hands.

Were he to destroy this piece of paper, George would be a wealthy man. The foolish feeling he had come to have for the boy tempted him. He reminded himself, shudderingly, of what George would do with the money: the building of the clinic, and a fund set up for treating the worthless, free of charge; and, one way or another, it'd be give, give, give, until the work of old Walt's entire lifetime had been frittered away. Impossible to contemplate. The prospect offended all his instincts. Provoked, he shoved the envelope to one side and turned to his accounting.

How long he worked he did not know. He heard only the sighing of the fire and the punctual calling of the cuckoo clock from the kitchen. So, when he looked up and saw the man in the red sweater standing there, he was completely taken aback. Not afraid, exactly, but surprised and angry.

"What the hell do *you* want?" he blurted out, getting to his feet.

"The keys to the car in the garage out there," said the man outrageously.

Such unholy disregard for privacy and property floored

the old man. "Why—what—you mean, you want a lift to someplace?"

"That's right, Pop. Only I'll do my own driving. Where are the keys?"

Old Walt became intensely conscious of the emptiness of the house, of the money littering the desk, of the gun rack not three feet behind the intruder's shoulder. "I don't hand out the keys to my car, mister," he said firmly. "Now you go along about your business, if you know what's good for you."

His fingers, creeping toward his pocket, had betrayed him. Quick as a striking snake, the man lunged for the coat pocket and came up with the keys. "Like taking candy from a baby, Pop."

"I'll call my son!" old Walt said loudly. "I'll call my son and he'll—"

"Quit bluffing. I been watching. There ain't nobody else here. Do you think I'm a fool?" His black eyes glittered as he looked down at the desk. "Say, this is nice, real nice. Got any more of it in the house?" He began scooping the money up, stuffing it into his pockets.

Old Walt saw his chance and took it. He ran past the man to the gun rack, pulling down an army revolver, pointed it at the scoundrel's impudent back. "Now then," he said, panting. "Now then. Put that back where you found it. You—you thief!"

The man turned quickly and his eyes shone. "Guns!" he said softly. "What d'ya know! Guns." He actually took a step forward.

So unnerving was it to see pleasure where fear should have been that the old man hesitated. "Stay where you are! This is loaded. I warn you!" he called out desperately to the advancing enemy.

Then, terrifyingly, the room began to whirl. An excruciating pain shot through his left arm and gripped his chest. He felt himself toppling to the floor amidst a great roaring in his ears. Consciousness departed and returned intermittently, so that, lying there motionless, he saw his surroundings only in occasional flashes, as if a light switch were being flicked on and off. He knew that the strange man was taking an overcoat and a hat from the closet and putting them on. He saw the gun lifted from his impotent hand, to be jammed into the overcoat pocket. But when or how the man left he did not know.

There was a long gap, and then George was bending over him, his face distressed, his hands busy with a hypodermic needle. He wanted to ask George if the thief had been caught but he found it impossible to speak, and George, seeing his effort, forbade it.

"You mustn't move, Dad. Not a finger. Not an eyelash. I've put you on the couch here by the fire, and I'm wrapping you in a blanket. You have to stay warm and quiet while I run down to Yorks' and phone for an ambulance. Understand? I'll be gone just ten minutes. You *must* listen to me this time. Please."

Lying there alone, his mind began to collect itself. He had had a heart attack and he was going to die. The idea of death was so foreign to him that he nearly smiled at the absurdity of it. Well, not a bad way to leave the world, lying lazily here in this familiar room, watching the firelight dance on the walls. His eyes lingered on it all, like a child bidding his favorite toys good night. The old pictures. The big armchair. The desk.

The desk! A terrible urgency seized him. That white envelope lying there contained a foolish paper, drawn up in the days when he had been blind and ignorant. He loved George, there was no harm in admitting it now; and he wanted George to know it too. But suppose he should die before George got back? He must obviate that possibility. He was not going to deny himself this final pleasure of giving his son a present.

He rolled himself off the couch. Walking was beyond him, but he could creep. Painfully, stubbornly, he inched his way to the desk, pulled himself up the side of it, grasped the will in his hand. He had to get close to the fireplace to make sure of his aim, but it was very near, and the paper was obedient. It fluttered into the flames, and he lay on the hearth, contented, watching it burn.

He would have liked so much to tell George about everything: the intruder, the gun, the stolen car, and the present he had just given him. But time had run out. When he felt arms lifting him, he looked into his son's face and tried to say, "Good boy." The words were inarticulate. His head fell back against George's shoulder, and his pulse ceased.

Wentworth, a city of a hundred and fifty thousand souls, lies on the northwestern edge of Lake Michigan, in the state of Wisconsin. Summers, when the tourist season is under way, its population doubles. The little expensive shops reopen, the hotels import college students to augment their staffs, cabins and cottages are jammed, and hundreds of boats come to dance in the harbor. Winters, the town relapses into sedateness, like a conservative household that has survived the stay of a rich, hysterically gay relative. Snow fences go up along the roads and the town turns its back to the cutting wind off the lake and goes about its usual business at the dairy farm and boat factory.

Asked to name Wentworth's most prominent citizen, a native resident would reply unhesitatingly, "Mike Cassidy. You've heard of him? The big lawyer, goes all over the United States? Mike's a local boy, one of the smartest we ever had. Big shots from Cleveland and Chicago come looking for Mike when they need a good lawyer. No, I don't know him myself, except on sight. He doesn't mix much. Not like his brother Paul." A new enthusiasm would creep into the native's voice. "Have you met Paul Cassidy? Cap, we call him. Well, you will. He knows everybody and everybody knows him. Big friendly guy, honest as the day is long, takes a real personal interest in people. One of the finest athletes in the state, in his time. He's been our chief of police for the last ten years, and you won't find a better-run department anywhere!"

The average taxpayer in Wentworth had no idea that Cap Cassidy was about to lose his job. The people who knew it—a real estate man or two, the president of the bank, a big building contractor, two members of the City Council, Mayor Haynes, and Mike Cassidy—were keeping quiet about it, biding their time.

But Cap Cassidy was finding out. He had felt the first premonition on a day, months ago, when Mike dropped in at City Hall. Usually the brothers saw each other only on Cap's instigation. It was a bad sign when Mike came around on his own.

"Nothing special on my mind," Mike said, innocent-faced. "Have a few minutes to spare before I take the train to Chicago, thought I'd see how you were."

Cap admitted cautiously that he was fine, and Mike strolled about the office and talked about inconsequential matters. "Saw Laura downtown about a week ago. She tells me the youngsters have had the flu."

"A lot of it around." He knew there was something Mike wanted to say, and since he didn't come right out with it, he must be waiting for a cue. Carefully Cap introduced several likely subjects that fell flat. Then he said, "What's taking you to Chicago?" By the slight straightening of Mike's small wiry body, he knew immediately that he had given the proper line.

"Have a client there I'm handling some business for. Named Frescatti. Ever hear of him?"

"Angelo Frescatti? Sure, I've heard of him. Just like I've heard about the Capones and Bugsy Moran and—"

"Come now. Come now. He isn't quite that bad. You sound so *virtuous*, Paul."

He'd had a lifetime of Mike's little jeers and he took the tiny stings as a matter of course. "I've even *seen* him. On television, when the Kefauver Committee was getting evidence about gambling in Chicago. My private opinion is that he ought to be hanged. How did you happen to get mixed up with a crook like him?"

Mike was amused. "I warn you, you're talking libelously. There's no genuine proof that—well, no matter. I've just bought a hundred acres on the lake for him. Up along the bay where they thought they were going to have the municipal air field."

"What does Frescatti want property around here for?"

Mike shrugged. "He didn't say, precisely. I imagine, to build a hotel. I had to make a careful examination of possible restrictions on something of that sort."

"Hotel!" said Cap furiously. "Frescatti doesn't run hotels, he runs gambling joints. You'd better remind him that this state has laws about that kind of thing. He can't bring one of his dives in here!"

"Who says he can't?" said Mike softly.

"I do. I'll close him down the minute he opens!"

"I'm sorry to hear that. I am, really. In the first place, it's uncharitable of you to assume that the hotel will be anything more than just a hotel. In the second place, Mr. Frescatti is a very generous man to those who understand him. If you were to be realistic about this scheme of his you might find it—rewarding."

Cap got out of his chair. "Are you offering me a bribe? Did Frescatti tell you to—"

"He doesn't know you exist, Paul. Sorry. Your fame hasn't spread to Chicago. I was simply giving you some information for your own good. I see that my efforts were wasted." He looked greatly pleased. "I thought they would be."

Cap was left to puzzle over that last remark. From anyone else it might have been a compliment, but not from Mike, who had hated him since boyhood. Without cause, Cap would swear to that. Often, driven wild by his younger brother's spitefulness, Cap had yearned to knock him down, but he never had. Mike was five inches too short and forty pounds too light to be fair fighting game. There was nothing for it but to accept the perplexing situation and try to make allowances.

Cap's wife, Laura, said he made too many allowances. When they were first married, she refused to listen to his accounts of how brilliantly Mike was doing at the university. "Don't get your hopes up, Paul. He won't be any different when he comes home than he was before. It'll save you a lot of trouble if you stop trying to be friends with him."

"He's bound to outgrow his crankiness. You'll see."

"He won't outgrow being jealous of *you*."

He had to look at her twice to make sure she wasn't joking. "You're talking through your hat! He's a professional man, a lawyer, and I'm a policeman. What's he got to be jealous of?"

"I don't know. Being kid brother to a hero must be a hard thing to shake off."

"A hero!" he said with some of Mike's own disdain. "That's all past and done."

"Not for him." She laid her cheek against his shoulder. "In a way, he's right. You're a better man than he is. That's why I can't bear to see you putting yourself out for him, over and over again, and getting kicked in the teeth for your pains. You have a thousand friends. You don't *need* him."

"Mike doesn't care about people. With his brains, he doesn't *have* to care."

She sat up irritably. "I won't have you feeling inferior to him! That's what he'd like, that's what he's after. And

57

you mustn't trust him. He isn't honest. Not even with himself."

He laid most of this to wifely prejudice. Mike was devious but not dishonest. His professional reputation was impeccable. He couldn't be bought. To be fair to him, he didn't care particularly about money. So it was not like him to take Frescatti for a client. Why had he? Why did Mike want to visit Frescatti's interests on a town where he himself lived? How did he reconcile this with the fact that he was a leading member of the Wentworth Civic Crusaders and adviser to the Better Business Bureau? Personal power and the manipulation of people were the things Mike cared about, and it was difficult to see how Frescatti could help him there. Then what were his motives?

Cap let a few weeks pass and then went to Mayor Haynes. The mayor was a pudgy little man who diverted attention from thought by talking continuously. It was one of Cap's little jokes that he hated to ask the mayor a question for fear he might answer it.

Mayor Haynes launched into a happy monologue. "Yes, I've talked to Mike. He came around a few weeks back, to sound me out. All I can tell you is that we—the Council and myself—have the matter under consideration. Naturally I brought up some objections, but your brother assures me that they are invalid. He is certain that Mr. Frescatti wishes only to build a hotel—a *luxury* hotel, such as we do not have at present—and chose this location because it is the most beautiful in the state." He paused, but Cap did not take the opportunity to echo praises of the local scenery. The mayor resumed, defensively. "Well, a place like that might be an excellent thing for the town. Increase business, draw tourists. Mr. Prescott, over at the bank, is all for it. He—"

The chief said bluntly, "Mr. Prescott is thinking of the bank, I'm thinking of the town."

"Of course you are!" said the mayor approvingly. "And so am I. Mike pointed out, too, that if Mr. Frescatti exceeds the terms of the license we grant him we can always close him down. That'll put him on his good behavior, as it were. The risk isn't—"

"Once he opens, he'll stay open, you'll find. How do you suppose he keeps running in St. Louis and Los Angeles? The citizens don't want him, but he's going full blast."

The mayor shifted in his chair. "No need to get stirred up about it yet, Paul, seems to me. It's all a long way off. Mr. Frescatti may change his mind, the Council may not vote the permit—a lot of things can happen. Let's not cross our bridges until we come to them."

The signs of bridge-crossing appeared, soon enough. First, beginning nowhere, there was a ripple of excited gossip through the town. Then in quick succession Mike addressed the Chamber of Commerce and the Rotary and Kiwanis clubs. Businessmen began to look judicious and benign when the new hotel was mentioned. An alarming hint blew up that a site a hundred miles farther south was also under consideration. The Wentworth *Eagle* met this with an editorial: "Many people have called to inquire if Wentworth has lost the chance of playing host to the great hotel whose building is being contemplated by a Chicago corporation, represented locally by Michael Cassidy. As far as we can ascertain, there is no truth to the rumor. Mr. Forbes, president of the corporation, told us, when contacted in Chicago, that Wentworth is still the favored location, providing that various minor difficulties can be ironed out." By August, when the architect's drawings were displayed magnificently in the window of Stucky's hardware store, crowds gathered before them all day, eager, impressed. So expertly had the town been softened up that anyone who denounced the project, on any grounds at all, stood a grave chance of being called an obstacle to progress and an enemy of the people.

Hoping against hope, Cap went again to the mayor. "Frescatti's name isn't connected with the hotel any more. Has he dropped out?"

"I believe he's a member of the corporation. Just a member. Several of the biggest men in the Middle West are in it with him. Men of undoubted probity who—"

"Undoubted probity, my foot! Those boys are figureheads. Frescatti *owns* them."

The mayor's face flushed a bit. "I'm afraid you'll have to leave the handling of this matter to the city government, Paul. I appreciate your concern. No one is more interested in keeping Wentworth clean than *I* am, but—" But stop trying to throw a monkey wrench into the works, and go away.

Useless though he suspected it to be, Chief Cassidy began to build up a folder on Frescatti and his previous business ventures. At his own expense he drove to the state library and spent two days among the newspaper files, taking notes. The folder grew so bulky that it scarcely fitted into the drawer of his desk, where he carefully locked it away after each ensuing addition. He indicated to Mayor Haynes that he had some pertinent information about Frescatti that His Honor should see, and this time the mayor told him firmly that he was out of his province.

All he could do, after that rebuff, was to consider the plight of the chief of police of Wentworth, once Frescatti was entrenched. That official would have to close one eye, grant special favors, overlook the presence of men listed in his files as criminal or undesirable, and help cover up the messes that threatened unfortunate publicity. Money would pass into complacent palms until the whole arm of the law was paralyzed. A hopeless and untenable situation.

The prospect depressed him to such an extent that Laura threatened to call a doctor and several of his friends complained that he had cut them dead on the street. Only Avery, the brightest young man on the *Eagle,* came close to the truth. "If you aren't sick or in trouble at home, then you're holding out on me. Have a heart, Cap. Spill it." But there was no use in telling Avery. Mr. Hoiles, who owned the *Eagle,* was solidly on Mike's side.

In September he impulsively wrote out his resignation, to take effect on the last day of the year. "In the light of present circumstances, I believe it will soon be impossible to discharge my duties as chief of police properly and to the satisfaction of the mayor and the Council, therefore I . . ." He left the letter on the mayor's desk before he went home that night.

It was harder to tell Laura than he had thought. He stood before the upstairs mirror while he changed his clothes, and the reflection in the glass disturbed him. From a distance he looked like a husky young fellow; there were no pouches under his eyes, no gray in his hair. But, closer up, he saw the telltale slackness under the jaw, the lines that stayed even when the face was composed. He was forty-seven years old. What kind of new job could you get at forty-seven? His whistling, as he ran down the stairs, was not as cheerful as he would have liked.

The news was far more than Laura had bargained for. "You shouldn't have!" she wailed. "Oh, Paul, is it too late to get that letter back?"

"I don't want it back. I'll find something else to do. A situation like that would drive me crazy."

"But you've played right into their hands. Don't you see? You've done just what Mike *wanted* you to do!"

"Don't blame my resignation on Mike. He had nothing to do with it."

"Oh, didn't he? Why did he jump at the chance to let this—gangster—loose on the town? Why did he make a special visit, first thing, to tell you about it? Because he knew you wouldn't be able to stomach it, that's why!"

Downhearted as he was, he had to laugh. "You believe that Mike went to all this trouble just to make me quit? That this million-dollar deal was all for *my* benefit? I'd be flattered if I could think so."

"He knew you'd never believe it! For half a cent I'd call him up myself and—"

He forbade that. "He'd laugh at you, Laura. I won't let you make a fool of yourself."

"No. You'd rather let him get away with making fools of all of us. I know." And, though she hugged him tenderly a minute later, he was left with an impression that he had failed her in some mysterious fashion.

The mayor paid him a call the next morning, bearing

the letter in his hand and looking grieved. "You don't mean this, my boy. A hasty, ill-considered action. We all make them. What do you say we tear it up, here and now?" Even in the face of refusal, he would not concede the matter settled. "Maybe you need time to think it over, Paul. I won't show this to the Council until—oh, the first of December. Meanwhile, we won't say a word about it, to anybody. Then, if you reconsider, as I'm sure you will, there'll be no awkwardness about your simply keeping on. No explanations, no newspaper stories—"

"That's very good of you, but—"

The mayor waved a magnanimous hand. "You've nothing to thank me for. I'm glad to go along with you, just as far as I possibly can."

Which was pretty decent of the old codger, any way you looked at it.

In October great shipments of lumber and steel began pouring into town. The second week in November the *Eagle* printed a regretful item: "Mr. and Mrs. Michael Cassidy have recently purchased a home in Cleveland, Ohio, and have announced that they will take residence there by next April. The move is necessitated by Mr. Cassidy's business interests. We wish them bon voyage and an eventual return."

Cap read this at four o'clock in the afternoon. At four-ten he walked into his brother's law office, ready to say a thing or two about rats and sinking ships, but the secretary said that Mike was out of town. "I'm sure he'll be sorry to have missed you, Mr. Cassidy. His wife happens to be here, just stepped in for a minute. Would you care to talk to her?"

"Well, no, I—"

But Olga had heard his voice. "Is that you, Paul? Come on in."

She was sitting at Mike's desk leafing through a big scrapbook, and her smile for him was genuine. Childless herself, she had frequently borrowed one of his three youngsters for a picnic or a movie, but she hadn't done that for a long time now. Interested in other things, likely. Club work or shopping sprees. He had an idea that her dress was extremely stylish. She had always borne her loneliness picturesquely and with dignity.

"Why don't you age a little?" he said. "You're making the rest of us look conspicuous."

"Lovely man!" She pointed to the scrapbook. "Look what I found on Mike's desk. Speaking of aging, here's your lost youth."

He turned the heavy pages slowly. Every picture was of himself: at ten, scowling out from beneath the visor of a baseball cap; at fifteen, in football harness; at seventeen, accepting the County Tennis Tournament Singles Cup. The clippings, crisp with age, detailed each achievement of his, no matter how small or long-forgotten: the day he had pulled two half-drowned vacationers out of the lake; the award for being voted Best All-Around Boy in the senior class. (He knew now what happened to Best All-Around Boys. They ended on the ash heap at fifty.)

"Where did all this come from?" he said wonderingly.

"Mike must have saved it. I've never seen it before, didn't dream you'd been so famous."

He closed the book and his voice was harsh. "Guess Mike kept it for laughs."

"Why would he? There's nothing funny about it."

"Mike does strange things."

She considered this, tilting her head reflectively. "And you've never tried to stop him," she said almost absently. "Have you?"

"I learned a long time ago that there's no stopping Mike once he gets the bit between his teeth."

"I think he *can* be stopped. Oh, not without a struggle. More of a one than I could put up. But *you* might be a match for him, if you cared to be."

Her tone was light and friendly, and he suppressed the resentment he had begun to feel. "A lot of bickering and brawling, that's what it'd take. I won't stoop to it."

"Too proud to fight. I see." She took his arm, laughing as if there were some joke that they both understood. "Well, I guess one excuse is as good as another."

He left her at the curb where her car stood and walked back to the City Hall. The clock in the Methodist steeple tolled five, but he didn't want to go home until he was calmer. The scrapbook and Olga had upset him. There was an unwanted tension in his nerves and muscles, a physical sensation of needing to run or fight, or both. If he ate dinner feeling like this, he'd be sick.

In the outer office the police stenographer handed him a note. "This just came in for us, sir. It's marked urgent."

"Thanks, Bill. Have you looked up this Norris in the files yet? I'd like to see what we have on him."

"I'll do that, right away. Mr. Avery from the *Eagle* is inside, waiting for you."

"Good. Call my wife and tell her I won't be home for dinner, will you? Think I'll stick around awhile."

Avery greeted him enthusiastically. "Say, Cap, I've had a brain storm. Should have had it a long time ago. I'd like to do a big feature story on you!"

He liked Avery. His good humor was restored. "Going to make a little go a long way?" he asked indulgently.

Avery scowled. "None of this modesty business, please. I'm after facts. You're the worst public relations man in the world, but I'm going to make you famous in spite of yourself."

It turned out that Avery had a friend on a Milwaukee paper that was running a series on Wisconsin's Outstanding Citizens. "You know, people who haven't been publicized but have a strong influence on their communities. Well, take all this work you do with delinquent kids, for one thing. The principal of the high school says that you—"

The record from the files was delivered. "Just a second, Avery. I have to take a look at this."

"Something come up? I hope."

"A convict escaped from the Michigan State Prison Farm about an hour ago. That's in the Upper Peninsula, about a hundred miles from us. They're alerting all points."

Avery came to look over his shoulder. "Bad medicine, hey? A real tough hombre. Maybe I'd better stay downtown tonight. Hoiles is in Florida, and if this guy heads our way—"

"A hundred miles across fairly open country is a long way to come without being caught. It's more likely he'll stay on the Michigan side, mix in with a bunch of deer hunters, and try to get the boat across the Straits."

Avery went back to his chair and began scribbling rapidly in a small notebook. "God knows, nothing exciting has happened around here since that farmer murdered his wife, back in 1950. If he does come this way and you get him, it'll make a wonderful finale for my feature story."

Cap looked silently at the bent head and the hurrying pencil. He had planned to stall Avery along until events themselves showed the young man that he had chosen unwisely in the matter of Wisconsin's Outstanding Citizens. But now he felt a twinge of pity. The Big Story. The Happy Ending. How young a man had to be to believe in those! "There isn't going to be a feature story," he said slowly. "Not about me."

The fat was in the fire then, with a vengeance. No one denied Avery something without explaining why. He rattled questions like a machine gun until the chief, cut off from evasion, confessed his impending resignation. The admission was not enough. Avery wanted reasons, probed for them, got nowhere, reached for his hat. "I'm going up to your house and have a talk with your wife," he said. "She's probably just as sore about this thing as I am. She'll talk."

Reluctantly Cap unlocked the desk drawer and brought out the Frescatti folder. "For your own information, then. Otherwise, this is in strictest confidence."

By eight o'clock he had told the whole story, citing chapter and verse, and Avery sat immobile, mulling it over. When he finally spoke his voice was respectful. "They put it over smooth as clockwork, didn't they? The people in town who'd buck the thing won't hear about it until it's too late. Very clever. Lots of brains behind a scheme like this."

"Mike's."

"I suppose. He's a real spellbinder, that boy. Has the mayor in his pocket obviously."

"I'm not so sure about *that*. Haynes is trying to be fair. The way he stalled off my resignation shows—"

"What a babe in the woods you are!" said Avery cynically. "Stop trying to attribute fine, righteous motives to politicians. They don't have 'em."

"He knows I'm against the deal, but he wants me to keep on being police chief anyway. How do you explain that if—"

Avery slapped a hand down on the desk. "I'll tell you how I explain it! Haynes wants you to resign, all right, but not now, not till the whole thing's ironclad. He's keeping you under wraps because he's afraid of you! You're well thought of. Too many people know you're a square shooter. What if you were to open your face and spill all this stuff you've told me? Do you think this precious deal would go through then? No, sir. And the mayor knows it." His shrewd eyes softened a little as he stared at the older man. "Though if he knew you just a bit better he'd be resting easier. You're not the kind to raise a public stink. Even a *healthy* public stink."

For the second time that day Cap felt that he had been weighed and found wanting, and indignation boiled up in his voice. "One person isn't enough to stop this thing. Suppose I went around to the men's clubs, the way Mike did, do you know what they'd say? 'Paul Cassidy's afraid he's going to lose his job and he's out hustling to keep it.'

That's all the effect I'd have, and they'd grin behind their hands. No, thanks. I'm not going to make a martyr or a laughingstock out of myself, either one!"

"Well, don't get sore at me," said Avery mildly. "I'm not telling you what to do. If I owned the newspaper I'd give you a helping hand. As it is, I can't even *talk* about it to anyone. Hoiles would fire me in a minute and right now I need the job." He stood up, buttoning his overcoat. "Funny, the things that keep people in line. I'm afraid of losing my job. You're afraid of being laughed at. Two of a kind."

"For God's sake, Avery, you're talking as if we were a couple of cowards! There's such a thing as common sense, you know!"

Avery winked at him. "Well, if you decide not to be sensible and go on a crusade, let me know. I'm feeling a little reckless these days. I might join you just for the hell of it."

The chief resisted a childish impulse to hurl the folder against the door that Avery closed behind him. Fuming, he threw it back into the drawer and wished that he had a milk of magnesia tablet. His stomach, usually an amiably efficient organ, could not digest this silly talk about crusading.

Joe, the night dispatcher, came in. "New bulletin on that escaped convict. The Michigan police report that he tried to get a girl to drive him here. She got away and he made off in her car. They think he might be making for our depot, to board a train for Chicago."

With action in the offing, he became excited and absorbed. He sifted every fact out of the new report: the old red sweater Norris was wearing, the make and license number of the car, the exact spot where the girl had abandoned it. While Joe called some of the day men back to duty, Cap plotted the road blocks and alerted his patrol cars. "Norris may have left the Ford by now and be on foot or hitching a ride. Stop any man who answers his description. Better to bring in ten innocent men than to let him slip by. He was unarmed at last report, but he is dangerous. Don't fool with him. *Stop* him."

He telephoned the ticket agent at the railroad station. The train for Chicago made up at Winnipeg, Canada, cut across the northern edge of Minnesota, pulled into Wentworth at ten-thirty, was on its way again at ten-thirty-five. Tonight it was running dead on schedule.

Cap took his gun from the top of the filing case and strapped it on under his suit coat. It had been a long time since he had worn it, and it felt good. "I'll cover the depot myself," he said to Joe. "If they should nail Norris beforehand, call me there."

As he pulled his car out of the deserted police garage, the clock on the dashboard registered nine-forty. Usually a couple of his men sat near the entrance, swapping stories and trying to keep their feet warm while they waited for emergency calls. Tonight they were all out, patrolling the town, looking for a tall thin man in an old red sweater. And if they missed him it was up to the chief to provide the final, insurmountable barrier to the fugitive's escape. The way he figured, it was only fitting and proper that the last responsibility should be his.

The station platform was long and floodlights lit the center portion of it in front of the main entrance to the

The Frightened Ones

old-fashioned inadequate building. The pavement here was of ancient brick with a raised curb marking the twelve-inch drop to the railroad tracks. As he parked his car in the fringe of darkness, where two empty taxicabs stood, he was in the position of a man sitting in a theater and looking up at a lighted stage where players moved about. In this case the players were a group of teen-agers, milling and laughing, their coats open to the wind, their heads bared to the snow. There were a dozen of them and he heartily wished them a thousand miles away. If Norris came, these too-emotional girls and these incautious boys were the very kinds of bystanders to make things tough. They would have to be protected, not only from gunfire, but from their own reckless impulses. He debated sending them home, but he'd have to give them a reason. Then give them five minutes to get to the Sugar Bowl or the nearest telephone, and half of the town might come trooping down! No, he'd have to let them stay.

They came to greet him the minute he stepped into the lights. He knew them all and his banter was knowing and friendly. He pretended to believe that they were all skipping town at once, and while they explained that they were only waiting to meet two "real cool" Canadian boys who were coming in on the ten-thirty, his eyes surveyed the waiting room through the station window and discovered no one but the two cab drivers, also known to him, warming their hands at a radiator. "Have to talk to the ticket agent a minute," he said. "If anyone shows up out here while I'm inside—anyone you don't know—come in and tell me, will you? I'm expecting to meet a man here."

He was talking to old Mr. Gillis at the ticket window

71

when young Louise Rickard stuck her head in at the door. "Man's here," she said.

He was at the door in three leaps before he heard their laughter and knew it was a joke. There was a man, but it was only Avery. "This is a stranger?" he said to them, and allowed Avery to pull him off to one side.

"Went back to headquarters on the off chance and hit the jackpot," Avery said. "Nothing doing here yet, I take it?"

"No. Chances are, there won't be."

"Pessimist! I've been talking long distance to the Michigan authorities and I've got quite a story ready to roll. This boy Norris *can't* fail me now."

"When a man's working by trial and error, as he is, you can't count on anything."

"Is there anywhere north of us where he could get this train?"

"No."

"Any place where it slows down and he could ride the rods or something like that?"

"Gillis says the train is small until they add on some cars farther south, and the crew police it pretty well."

"But if he managed to get aboard and they didn't know who he was, he could buy a ticket from the conductor?"

"Yes."

Avery looked at his watch. "She'll be along in ten minutes. I think I'll go call your office again. Something new might have come in."

"Help yourself."

He decided to make a brief turn of the far end of the

platform where he had not been. The high school kids were standing out near the tracks now, facing the way the train would come, and they did not notice him. He walked along close to the building and then halfway around it, looking into every shadow, peering behind each crate. Satisfied, he took his hand off his gun, leaving his overcoat open. There was a place where, standing in darkness, he could look down the entire length of the platform. A good enough vantage point for waiting.

Under his feet the pavement trembled, and far away the train whistled. Expectancy animated the entire depot. The two drivers came out and went to their cabs. Avery appeared and looked around. He was followed by a clerk carrying a leather mailbag, and the two of them stood and talked. The oncoming train grew noisier and the girls shrieked and put their hands over their ears. The chief, leaning toward the light, watched them all.

He saw the black shiny car drive up and park neatly beside his own. A Lincoln. Not new but well kept. No one got out. Someone waiting to take a passenger home with him? Still, he didn't know anyone in town who owned a black Lincoln like that one. From this distance there was no chance of identifying the driver. Inconspicuously, he began edging his way down the platform, using the din of the nearing locomotive as a time signal.

The train rushed into the station, enveloping everything in a smoky haze. A Pullman porter swung out and set a wooden platform in place for the disembarking passengers. The conductor appeared, waving the converging young people back. There was a confusion of sounds and voices, and the little crowd, having received the new arrivals, began bearing them away by slow inches. Ensconced in a dark angle near the parking area, Cap cursed their lack of speed. Couldn't they walk and talk at the same time? When the conductor called out, "All aboard!" they were still on the platform, all screaming and giggling at once.

The door of the Lincoln opened and a tall thin man in a respectable overcoat and a felt hat, tipped against the wind, got out. He moved purposefully toward the train, and so rapidly that Cap had just time to intercept him. He lunged forward and let the man run into him. "I'd like to see your driver's license," he said.

The man stepped back from the collision, glancing obliquely from beneath the hatbrim. "Listen, I'm in a hurry. Some other time."

Cap produced his badge, keeping his other hand on the gun in its holster. "The driver's license. Now."

The man's two hands came out of his pockets. In one was a sheaf of money, in the other a gun. "Which'll it be?" he said. "Take your choice."

Cap stared down at the weapon, marveling at his own stupidity. He hadn't expected such boldness and, in spite of his warnings to his men, he had counted too heavily on the authority of his badge. Now there was only one way out and he sighed, regretting the way, regretting many things.

The train's wheels gave a preparatory jerk. Norris trembled with impatience, but he was careful to keep his face away from the light and the chief's bulk between himself and the chattering kids. "You don't have to worry about taking the dough," he urged. "Some of my friends passed me the word this is a safe town. That's why I made for it. Play ball, for God's sake! Be smart."

With one hand Cap reached for the money. With the other he drew his gun and shot Norris a careful three inches above the heart. The convict fell, and the wind lifted the paper bills and swirled them after the departing train.

Cap turned and looked at the young people, huddled in dismay. "Go on home," he said gently. "Everything's going to be all right."

Avery came running up, delirious with excitement. "What happened? I went back in to the phone, and I heard the shot—" He stared down at the gun in the convict's relaxed hand. "Did he pull a gun too? Did he use it?"

"He tried to. I don't know what happened that he didn't. Something wrong with the gun, maybe. Call the Meyersville ambulance, will you? I'll stay here till they come."

"You bet." He took a few steps and returned, to shake the chief's hand. "You're a real hero, Cap. I'm proud to know you."

"Wait until tomorrow. The real heroics start then." He touched Norris lightly with his foot. "We can't have this. I've made up my mind."

"Crusading?"

"Yes."

"Count me in."

"Thanks."

A safe town. Win or lose, he was going to try for that.

Newspapers everywhere printed the story of the capture. The following, taken from one of the Detroit papers, is as accurate as any.

WENTWORTH POLICE CHIEF STOPS CONVICT
FUGITIVE WOUNDED IN GUN BATTLE AT DEPOT

Jake Norris, convicted thief and suspected murderer, who escaped from the Altman Prison Farm yesterday, is in Meyersville Hospital recovering from a wound incurred in a gun battle with Paul Cassidy, chief of police of the city of Wentworth. Norris, supposedly unarmed, drew a gun first and attempted to fire. Later, police discovered that his gun, though otherwise in good condition, contained very old ammunition. The source of the gun has not yet been traced.

Norris was apprehended as he was about to board a train for Chicago. Mayor Haynes of Wentworth later issued a statement of commendation of Chief Cassidy "whose brave action saved the lives of our townspeople and prevented a menace being let loose on the country at large."

The first report of the route of the fleeing Norris came from Mrs. Elizabeth Stevens, a widow, at whose Michigan farm Norris seized a sweater and a bicycle. His attempt to take some money was foiled by Mrs. Stevens' son John, who forced the convict to flee.

Later Norris stopped a car driven by Miss Ella Mack of Black Corners and demanded to be driven across the state line to Wentworth. Miss Mack escaped and notified the police. Her car, with two flat tires, was discovered ten miles further on, parked on the shoulder of Route 62 in the lake area.

When Norris arrived at the railroad station he drove a black Lincoln sedan. Its license plate was missing and mud had been rubbed on the back of the car to conceal this. Police believe he secured the car from a house whose owners were away. No such car has been reported as missing. Doctors say it will be several days before Norris can be questioned.

"Norris is a thoroughly bad character," says Lieutenant Harris of the Michigan State Police, "We are fortunate that his attempted escape had no serious consequences, except to himself."

Second Chance

Mr. Brown often said that if there was one place where a man was entitled to a little peace and quiet it was at home. He said that after a hard day of making the decisions that an executive had to make—going over accounts, checking the work of salesmen, dictating letters that would spur the buying of valves and pipe in cities hundreds of miles away—a man's torn mind needed the healing of complete relaxation. His own house, when Mr. Brown was in it, was as hushed as a cathedral.

This happy domestic state was not an accident. It was the result of Mr. Brown's methodical training of his family. In the early days of his marriage his wife Ellen had been inclined to protest. "I don't mind staying home, Norman, but all you want to do is to sit and read your newspaper and then go to bed. You don't even *talk* to me."

He had been kind but firm. "If I'm to get anywhere with the company I have to conserve my energies for the most important part of my day."

"The most important part of your day ought to be when

you're home, shouldn't it? Your work is just what you do for a living."

"That's typically a woman's remark, my dear. After all, my only thought is to make things more comfortable for you."

"Well, can't you *talk* to me while you're doing it?"

His sigh rustled the newspaper. "I've been talking all day."

Ellen folded her lips. "I haven't," she said shortly, and went back to the kitchen to do the dishes.

After the babies were born he was forced to mention over and over again that noise and confusion paralyzed his working faculties and disoriented his thinking. Ellen ought to be able to set up a schedule that would have the babies suppered and in bed by the time he was ready to dine. And the children should be taught to mind! He didn't like to sit alone at the table while she bounced up and down, heeding calls from the nursery for drinks of water and good night kisses. Once they were in bed, that should end it! "You're not firm enough with them. I hate to think what would happen if I ran my office the way you run this house and the people in it."

"If the people in your office were all aged four and two, they might give you a little trouble." Her hands were too thin, he saw her rings slide loosely as she pushed back her hair. "Even you," she said.

Once, when Ted was five, Mr. Brown had lost patience. The crying and whimpering from upstairs made eating impossible. He threw down his napkin and rose. "I've had enough of this! If that child thinks he's going to carry on like that all night—"

"He has half a degree of temperature, Norman, he's coming down with something. I'm going up to him as soon as you've finished."

"Half a degree of temperature! More likely just an excuse to keep you waiting on him hand and foot. I'm going upstairs and settle that young man once and for all!"

He had made three thundering strides toward the door when Ellen's voice, cold and small, stopped him. "Come back, Norman."

The indignity of receiving such a command made him turn, his mouth full of angry words. He never said them. What he saw extinguished his rage and left him in a state of shock. Ellen was standing by her chair, one hand grasping the neck of a heavy cut-glass decanter as if it were a club. There was a half-smile on her face and her eyes were glittering, not quite sanely.

"Come back, Norman." The words barely stirred the air, but the threat behind them was infinite. With what dignity he could muster, he resumed his place at the table. Full of incredulous disapproval, he ate his pie, drank his coffee, kept his eyes away from her face until a strangled sound made him look up. She had her handkerchief to her lips, and for a moment he hoped for the decency of tears.

"If you're going to cry, please leave the table," he said bitterly. "I've put up with all I'm going to."

"I'm laughing," she said. "I'm laughing because anyone looking in that window would think we were a contented pair having a pleasant dinner. That's terribly funny!"

"I don't see anything funny about it. Nine evenings out

of ten, that's what we *are.*" He had not meant to dignify the scene she had made by referring to it, but the question blurted itself out before he could stop it. "What were you going to do with that decanter?"

"I was going to throw it at you, Norman." I was going to mend your socks. I was thinking of baking a lemon pie. Like that, calmly, factually, with no hint of respectable apology. "I don't mind suffering for my own mistakes, but I don't intend that the children shall suffer too."

For a long time that last remark disturbed him whenever he recalled it. Eventually he dismissed it as nonsense, as the foolish talk of a distraught woman.

In the twelve years that had gone by since then, there had never been a recurrence of her unseemly behavior. With maturity she had improved remarkably, becoming a really competent housekeeper, acquiring serenity in place of youthful rebelliousness. Charlotte and Ted had turned into well-behaved, well-mannered young people. Mr. Brown congratulated himself on the way he had molded his family and sometimes regretted that his appointment to a vice-presidency caused him to travel so frequently away from home.

When he was asked to dine at the houses of his out-of-town colleagues he could not help feeling superior. The gay, irresponsible wives they always had! The noisy, brawling, restless children! The careless demands on the businessman of the household! Father had to sponsor a scout troup, Father had to drive the whole family out for a picnic, Father had to pick Sally up after her dental appointment. It was unbelievable that these otherwise practical men would put up with such exactions. Mr.

Brown always pointed out, tactfully, that his family took care of all that kind of thing themselves. The businessmen grinned. "How do you get away with it?" they asked him. It was a silly question.

This particular evening, the one on his return from five days in Cleveland, he was savoring everything afresh. His dinner had been excellent. In the mirror over the buffet he caught sight of himself and his family, and he was pleased at the picture they made: Ellen, tall and patrician, with her ashblond hair piled becomingly on top of her head; Charlotte, handsome and dark, the very picture of this year's college girl; Ted, broad-shouldered and seventeen, keeping his elbows off the table assiduously; and himself, a good-looking man who did not need glasses and whose hairline had barely begun to recede, sitting with dignity at the head of the table. Indulgently, he was moved to talk to them. The sound of his voice rose and fell, interspersed with soft monosyllables from Ellen and the slight rasp of Ted's restless feet on the heavy carpet.

After dinner he had the living room gloriously to himself. Ellen was busy in the kitchen, it being her husband's belief that household help, even though you could well afford to hire it, was bound to bring idleness and discontent into your home. The kids had run off somewhere. He picked up his newspaper, but he was too contented to read. He listened to the spring rain awash on the windows and thought fleetingly of the neat legs of Miss Parrish, his stenographer. The unwonted appearance of his wife made him start guiltily.

"Yes?" he said gruffly.

Ellen spoke without looking at him, her fingers busily knotting an apron about her waist. "I have to be away for the next ten days, Norman. Dr. Johnson says I need an operation and we've arranged it for tomorrow. There was no use telling you before, you'd only have been upset. The children know."

The rain sounded louder to him. "Operation? What kind of operation?"

"A tumor, he says." She smiled deprecatingly. "There's a chance of malignancy, but then they always say that. It's too bad you haven't a trip coming up. I'm afraid things won't be too comfortable here for you. Mrs. Sheridan is coming in to take care of the house. She isn't perfect, but I was lucky to get her."

He felt his dinner settle into a hard lump in his stomach. "Haven't you—haven't you been feeling well?"

"Quite well. It's one of those things that can happen to you without your knowing it."

She went quietly back to the kitchen, leaving him rigid in his chair, his mind racing round like a caged squirrel. She couldn't be very sick, he'd have noticed it! Of course they had separate rooms—he had found he rested better that way—and for a long time now there had been no great physical intimacy between them. That was the way it should be, he didn't care for ardent women. Men wondered about girls like Miss Parrish, but they didn't marry them. A proper aloofness was an excellent quality in a wife. He had encouraged it in Ellen. Yet, if there was something so terribly wrong with her, he should have noticed it.

He walked out to the kitchen and stood in the doorway, watching her pour hot water over the dishes in the rack. "Don't do that," he said suddenly.

She had been thinking of something else. Her eyes came around to him slowly. "Don't do what, Norman?"

"Don't bother finishing up. Oughtn't you to be resting?"

"I'm going to bed as soon as I've finished. Charlotte wanted me to leave the dishes for her, but she has a night school class, and Ted had to go to basketball practice. They'll be tired when they get home." She folded the dishcloth neatly and hung it up. "Well, that's that," she said.

As soon as she had gone upstairs, he called Dr. Johnson. "About Ellen," he said. "How bad is she?"

"Can't tell. We'll do a frozen section right afterward, but we may have to send away for confirmation. We don't have a full-time pathologist here. The real answer won't come back for about three days."

"But it can't be going to be too bad. She seems—"

"I know. She makes a great business of keeping cheerful. Some years ago I recommended that she see a psychiatrist, but she seems to be working out her own adjustment."

"Psychiatrist! Do you mean to tell me that you thought that Ellen—"

"I believed it might help her. She's an exceptionally repressed and frustrated person, and—"

"I don't know what you're talking about," said Mr. Brown flatly.

The doctor's voice took on a slight edge. "I'm saying

that your wife is a fine woman and that it's a shame that human beings are so perishable. Both of which you know as well as I."

Mr. Brown went back to the empty living room and stared wretchedly at the darkness outside. He had wanted reassurance and the lack of it had increased his sense of foreboding. When, by the splinters of street light through the rain, he saw Ted come running down the street, he was glad. For the first time in his life he felt the need of his son's company. He waited until Ted crossed the living room, making for the stairs. Then he cleared his throat. "Fine weather for ducks," he said awkwardly.

"Oh. Dad. I didn't see you." His haste, his vitality had vanished. He stood there, politely.

"Maybe you should have missed basketball practice tonight. Your mother—"

"She wanted me to go, sir."

"Oh, well then." He didn't want to ask Ted to sit down, but couldn't the boy see that a little sociability was in order? "Shame you had to get soaked. You should have taken the car."

"You said I wasn't to drive the family car till I was twenty-one, sir."

Staggered, Mr. Brown recalled that he had several times been vehement on the subject. Now that he was looking at Ted's alert face, the ultimatum seemed a little silly. "Maybe we ought to get you a car of your own." That'd fetch him! All high school boys were crazy about cars.

Ted smiled vaguely. "Thanks, but I'd rather not. I get along all right this way. If I had a car of my own there'd be a lot of rules and regulations about it and not enough money for gas and—well, there'd always be a lot of trouble about it. Thanks anyway. Good night, sir."

He was gone, leaping catlike up the stairs. Evidently he stopped at his mother's door, for Mr. Brown heard his clear voice drifting down. "Hiyah, baby. Book any good?" Once Mr. Brown would have shouted up the stairs that that was no way for a boy to speak to his mother. But in his present state of loneliness he saw nothing wrong with it. It was infinitely better than being called sir, like a prep school master.

He thought that he might have a little talk with Ellen himself, but her room was dark when he passed it, a foreign citadel that he could not bring himself to invade. He undressed and went to bed, but he did not sleep. He heard a car door slam, and Charlotte's voice mingled softly with a young man's. Then the car drove off and Charlotte came upstairs so gently that only a movement of fabric betrayed her. Confidently she went into her mother's darkened room and closed the door. After that the house was very quiet.

He had always hated hospitals, the smell of them, the rows and rows of rooms where the sick and maimed and useless lay. There was, he had often said, no excuse for visiting them; if a person was sick enough to be in a hospital he was too sick for visitors. Even when Ellen had been in the maternity ward he had seen her only once. "Plenty of time to see you and the baby afterward," he had said. "Matter of fact they oughtn't to let outsiders into a place like this. It interferes with their work. It's inefficient." And there was the inconvenience of eating a hurried dinner and getting back out into the weather, just to spend an hour with someone who would soon be home anyway. All foolishness.

But this gray spring morning he stayed on, though they had told him it wouldn't do any good, he might as well go on about his business, his wife wouldn't even be conscious before evening. It was noon before they wheeled her out of the surgery and he had a glimpse of a white waxen face resting on white linen. The young, unborn look of it frightened him. He grabbed the doctor's sleeve.

"How'd it go? Have they run the test yet?"

"They've run it. As I told you, Mr. Brown, our test is not final but—well, it doesn't look too good. You have to be prepared for any eventuality."

"She isn't even forty yet," he said hoarsely. "It's impossible that she—"

"All we can do is wait for the pathologist's report. We may have nothing to worry about."

They wouldn't let him into her room, though he explained that he just wanted to sit there, he wouldn't be in the way.

"Better not," they said. "You go on to your office. It'll help take your mind off it."

The word "office" surprised him as much as if they had spoken it in Chinese. Office. Stubbornly he tried to tell them that this was no time to think about offices or sales charts or business hours, but they didn't listen. They had an incomprehensible jargon of their own. "These guilty husbands," he overheard one nurse say to another, "all over the place when it's too late in the day." She seemed

to be referring to him and, though the remark was sense-
less, it was annoying to feel that he was being discussed.

He went home, fuming, impotent, wretched. The house
felt cold and alien, with Mrs. Sheridan making an unholy
clatter in the kitchen. The papers from the night before
still lay on the rug by his chair, the flowers had wilted in
their vases. When he went upstairs his bed was unmade,
an unheard-of thing, and his room looked tousled.

But Ellen's room, when he tiptoed into it, was immaculate, the organdy spread crisp and neatly laid, the closet
doors tightly closed, a few tall bottles of cologne the only
articles on her dresser. It looked like a guest room, impersonal, inarticulate, transient. He threw himself down on
the bed, heedless of his clothes or the spread, and stared
at the picture on the bedside table. It was of Ellen and
the two children, and it had been taken many years ago.
He thought of the wax mask on the stretcher, and he
could not reconcile it with the face of this spirited young
matron, her narrow hands laid lightly on her children's
shoulders. Where had she gone, this girl in the picture?
And what had become of the two laughing children? He
did not know these people. They were strangers to him.
Then and now.

"My own fault," he whispered. "Oh, God, I see it now.
By my own fault, I am the loneliest man in the world."
The thought tortured him until, exhausted, he fell into a
comalike slumber.

It was dark when he was awakened by the ringing of
the telephone in the hall below. He heard Ted's voice
answering, and he rushed downstairs in a panic, rubbing
his eyes. Ted was just hanging up.

"The hospital?" Mr. Brown asked. His voice was a croak.

"Yes, they—"

"What did they—how is—"

"She's conscious. Dr. Johnson said she had been asking for me and Charlotte and that it would be all right for us to go over there a while."

"Fine. We'll all drive over together."

Ted looked down at his feet. "Well, Dr. Johnson said there could be only two visitors and that we could stay just a few minutes. And he thought that, since you had been there this morning, you wouldn't mind—"

Charlotte came up behind them, her hands clasped tensely. "You don't like hospitals anyway, Dad, you've always said so. And if Mother wants *us*—"

He said stonily, "Go ahead. It's all right."

He was too weary to argue. Not until they had gone did it occur to him that he should have told them to take the car. Well, a man as beset as he was couldn't be expected to think of everything!

Mr. Brown went to the office the next morning because there was no place else for him to go. He had expected that the familiarity of the place would act as a poultice to draw some of the pain out of him. Instead he found himself impatient with details and irritable with the pretty Miss Parrish.

"If you don't mind my saying so," he told her, "you are not dressed properly for an office of this kind. It is not necessary to look as though you were going to a tea."

Miss Parrish looked down at her black, tailored wool

and flushed. "I wouldn't wear this to a tea, Mr. Brown. Can you be more explicit?"

"All I know is the effect isn't businesslike. A little circumspection in these matters never goes amiss."

He saw that she was angry but he didn't care. The girl had been getting a bit above herself. Probably thought she was indispensable, and no one was that. Except, maybe, a man's wife and family. Mr. Brown was horrified to feel his vision blurring with unexpected tears, and he bent his head lower over his meaningless papers and struggled for composure.

By the time Jim Enderby came in for a conference about his new sales territory, Mr. Brown was once more straight in his chair. Enderby was an incompetent fellow, due to be fired. The records he submitted were right in line with Mr. Brown's opinion of him.

"It's no good, Enderby," he said. "It won't do. You can see that." His voice was more gentle than he had meant it to be.

It was all Enderby needed. He began to talk rapidly, unrestrainedly. His wife had been ill for so long, she'd always be an invalid. The children were farmed out among various relatives. It was hard to keep his chin above finantial disaster. And all these things affected his work, he couldn't stop thinking about them. He needed time to pull himself together, that was all. Time to get on his feet.

Ordinarily Mr. Brown would have made short work of him and these personal details that had no place in business. But he was in a queer, irrational mood today, ready to become emotional about anything. "Well, Jim," he said, "we'll give it another try. See what you can do by

next month." The remembrance of Enderby's blank, unbe-
lieving look of gratitude stayed with him all day. He
thought he might tell Ellen about Enderby.

Through the blue haze of late afternoon he went to the
hospital, his feet on the granite steps and the tiled corri-
dors as hasty as a lover's. Tall red roses stood in a vase in
the corner of Ellen's narrow room. The sight of them
stopped him in his tracks, impressed him with just how
cross he had made Miss Parrish. It was her duty to remind
him of things like sending flowers. Now she had failed
him deliberately so that he should be put in a bad light,
made to seem thoughtless and inconsiderate.

He tried to keep irritability out of his voice. "Well,"
he said. "Where'd the flowers come from?"

"The children sent them."

His joviality was restored. "Then I'll probably find them
charged to my account somewhere."

"Oh no. They paid for them out of their allowance. It'll
make them short, they shouldn't have done it, but"—she
breathed deeply—" the fragrance! When I close my eyes
I can believe I'm in a garden and not in a hospital at all."

"If they make you feel that good I'll have a truckload
sent around tomorrow."

She turned her head slightly in surprise. "You don't
need to, Norman. I'll be home in a few days and these will
last until then."

"Well, I suppose too many aren't practical."

She smiled, fleetingly. "No. Not practical."

He sat awkwardly on the edge of a wicker chair and
tried to find words to tell her that he realized that he had
been a selfish fool and that everything was going to be

different now. If she had encouraged him the least bit he might have managed; but she lay still, her head half averted, and Mr. Brown sat mute, feeling like a man whose hands were full of precious gifts that he was unable to give away. The silence grew so long that he thought that she might have fallen asleep, but when he leaned over to see she spoke.

"You might as well go home where you'll be comfortable, Norman. I'm feeling very well, and they'll be bringing in the supper trays shortly."

He went away, angry at his incapacity, frightened by her remoteness. She had lived at his elbow for almost twenty years, but he was as cut off from her as if a six-foot stone wall stood between them.

During the next thirty-six hours Mr. Brown's sensation of existing in a vacuum mounted to almost hysterical proportions. Ellen was going to die, he was sure of it, and he was going to be left stumbling about in an empty world, regretting forever the things he had not said and done. Frantically he tried to get closer to his children. "I haven't met your young man yet, Charlotte. Why don't you bring him in with you some afternoon?"

"There isn't any young man, Dad. Not any *one* young man."

"Well, bring home several of 'em. The place could stand some livening up. Don't young people have parties any more?"

"Oh yes. Mother's given a lot of them for us."

He stiffened. "I've never been in on one of them."

She said apologetically, "They're pretty noisy. And you're away a lot."

He had a sudden sense of the double life that his house led. Lights and noise and laughter and crowds when he was away, the front door slamming, voices calling from one room to another. And when he came home all the excitement and bustle going underground, leaving the solitude and vacancy that he had called peace.

It was too late for him to win Charlotte, he could see that. While he had been thinking of her as a child to be reprimanded and corrected, she had become a young lady who would shortly marry and move into a home of her own. There was no time left for him to establish a new relationship with her.

But Ted was younger. He'd be around home for the next five or six years, and Mr. Brown resolved to make every second count. He watched the boy's daily schedule like a hawk, so that he knew in just what few minutes he could corner him without seeming obtrusive about it. Before dinner was a good time.

"How'd practice go today, Ted?"

"Pretty well. We have a game Friday."

"There's a New York trip hanging over my head, but if I'm in town I'd like to come."

"Sure."

"I've never seen you play, you know."

"That's right."

Damnably hard sledding up the glassy politeness! "I s'pose the other fellows' families come. I'll have to make an effort."

"Mother comes quite often. And Uncle Bill's always there."

Mr. Brown winced. Ellen's brother Bill had never amounted to much, he'd had the same little accounting job all his life. Uncle Bill, indeed! "Haven't seen Bill in a long while," he said with false cordiality. "How is he?"

Ted became articulate. "He's fine. He's going to take a bunch of us camping for two weeks this summer, and he's just got his new car. Reason he's so glad, he said the old one'd never make the three hundred miles north." He threw back his head and laughed. "Not with six husky young guys packed into it. We told him in a pinch we could carry him and the car too."

"Evidently Bill has no trouble getting away from his job when he wants to."

"Oh, it's his vacation. He's taken us the last three summers. That's how I learned to drive."

He had to force his grudging lips. "I see. Well, that's mighty nice of Bill."

"Sure is. He's a real white man. You got to hand it to him."

"Next Friday I'll be at that game myself. That's a promise."

"That'll be fine, sir," said Ted indifferently.

"You don't sound very enthusiastic. Don't you want me there?"

"Sure I do. It's just—well, I think you *intend* to come, but—"

"But you don't think I'll make it."

Ted looked embarrassed. "All I'm going on is that you've

talked like this before, but you haven't made it yet. And I don't mind. I really don't. Oh, when I was a kid, I used to feel a little hurt about it, but I've outgrown all that."

"Well, it'll be different this time. You'll see." High time, too, that he took an interest in the boy. An unambitious man like Uncle Bill was bound to be a bad influence.

It had been established that Mr. Brown would visit his wife in the daytime and the children would go in the evening. Each afternoon, until he entered the doors of the hospital, he felt confident that this time the words would come, this time he would make Ellen aware of the happy change in him. And each afternoon, once beside her bed, he was gripped by a kind of stage fright that left him dumb and defeated. From these silent interviews he went home to the rank disorder of Mrs. Sheridan's housekeeping and tried to appear cheerful.

"Dinner ready, Mrs. Sheridan?"

" 'Twill be. How's Mrs. Brown?"

"Looking fine."

"Probably wore out as much as anything, poor soul. There's plenty of work in a house this size." She faced him, precariously defiant. "I sent the laundry out this week. I *had* to. Things was getting way ahead of me."

"That's all right, Mrs. Sheridan."

"How Mrs. Brown manages I don't know! I've worked in lots of places, but *this* one, without even a cleaning woman once a week to help—"

He went to bed early, worn out with these revelations of his past shortcomings, but sleep was beyond him. Wistfully he listened to the stirrings of Ted and Charlotte, studying late in their rooms. Once he heard a sob, but before he could rise Ted's footsteps went down the hall and his voice said, "What goes on here?"

"I've been thinking about Mother. Oh, Ted, what if she doesn't—"

"Here now, this won't do. You can't—"

Their voices sank, became inaudible.

Not once had the three of them talked together about the oncoming tragedy. The children had closed him out of their grief, apparently on the assumption that he did not share it; and their supposition that they had not even that much in common with him hurt, perhaps, the worst of all.

Dr. Johnson called him at his office the next morning. The belated report had just come in, there was no malignancy, Ellen would be as good as new very shortly.

The iron weight that had been compressing Mr. Brown's lungs lifted suddenly, and he sat breathing deeply for a while. Then firmly, quickly, he began sorting the papers on his desk. Lord, how he had let things slide!

"Call New York," he said to Miss Parrish. "Tell them I'm coming down over the weekend. See if you can get me reservations on the first plane Friday morning." Had there been something else he had planned to do on Friday? Well, whatever it was, it would have to wait.

"Mrs. Brown is better, then?"

"She's going to get well. They had us worried for a while." Miss Parrish remained impassive and he cleared his throat. "I suppose I've been pretty hard to live with these last few days. Sorry if I—"

Miss Parrish looked more friendly. "That's all right, Mr. Brown. Shall I check with the hospital about what day she'll get home and have flowers waiting there for her?"

"That'll be fine. You do that."

It was a pleasure to have such extraneous matters lifted from his mind. He settled down to business and had to be reminded that it was time for lunch and that Mr. Enderby would like to see him sometime that afternoon.

"Tell Enderby I haven't time. He has a month to make good and his figures can speak for him." By all that was holy, he had no intention of becoming a wet nurse for Jim Enderby!

At six o'clock he leaned back to ease his shoulder muscles and heard the silence in the outer office. No danger that any one of them would stay a minute longer than five-thirty. Not even Miss Parrish. Couldn't wait to run home.

He surveyed the two remaining hours of work that lay on his desk. It could be left, but loose ends were an abomination and he was going to be away. He reached for the telephone and then drew back his hand. No, to-night was a special occasion, he'd have to make a gesture. Best to go home, have dinner, drive the youngsters over to the hospital, visit with Ellen a minute, and then come back here and finish up. A foolish lot of extra effort for him, but it wouldn't take too much time and he had to eat dinner *somewhere*.

For once Mrs. Sheridan had the meal ready on the dot. Mr. Brown sat down, frowning. "That beef's been cooked too long," he said firmly. He explained in detail just how beef should be cooked while he took his time with the carving. Mrs. Sheridan vanished into the kitchen, sniffling, and he was pleased. Heretofore he'd been much too lax with her.

In high good humor, he ate a hearty dinner, admonishing Charlotte to do the same. Excitement was no excuse for picking at food. To Ted, who was eating tremendously as usual, he remarked that there was no hurry, they weren't going to a fire. As an example to them, Mr. Brown was slow and meticulous, and he felt the old, familiar annoyance with them when, the moment he had finished, they ran for their coats. In spite of all he had tried to teach them, they had no self-control. No self-control at all. He glanced longingly at the evening paper, lying folded beside his chair. First time in days that he'd relished his food, and he wasn't even to be permitted time for peaceful digestion. Still, there was no use putting his foot down, he had to get on to the office anyway.

The odor of the hospital halls, as they came in out of the spring night, smote him sickeningly. He said so to the children, but they only walked along, silent and unresponsive. "Don't swarm all over your mother when we go in," he cautioned them irritably. "Think of *her* a little, for a change."

Obediently enough, they stood at one side of the room while he walked over to the bed and kissed Ellen's cheek lightly. "Well, old girl," he said, "I hear there's not much wrong with you after all."

She was smiling past him, at her son and daughter. "No," she said. "The doctor says I'll be home next week."

"Mighty glad of it. Mrs. Sheridan is no jewel. We've missed you, all right. House all askew, terrible food—"

"There's no doubt that I'm a better housekeeper than Mrs. Sheridan," she murmured. "Is that what you've been trying to say to me all week?"

He was jocose. "Here I am trying to pay you a compliment and you sound disappointed. You women are never satisfied!"

She smiled briefly. "Aren't you going to take off your coat, Norman?"

"No, I have to get back to the office. Going to New York tomorrow. Thought you wouldn't mind since—"

"I don't mind at all."

Her voice sounded so cheerful that, for an instant, he was shaken. Was it possible that Ellen preferred his absence to his presence? Ridiculous! A peculiar idea like that was merely a hangover from his having been so upset all week, making mountains out of molehills, losing his whole perspective.

They said good night to him, Ellen calmly from the bed, Ted and Charlotte decorously from the two straight-backed chairs. He was almost out on the street when he realized that he had left his hat on Ellen's bedside table. Impatiently he made his way back to her room and opened the door.

The scene was no longer formal and correct, it was astonishingly lively. The three of them were close together, talking gaily, animatedly, their faces flushed with happiness. Then their heads turned, they saw him, there was an abrupt silence.

"Forgot my hat," he said. Nobody said anything. They just waited.

He went away, feeling obscurely angry, but the fresh

air of the parking lot restored him. As he got into his car Ellen and the children faded from his mind and his thoughts fastened sanely and strongly on the papers that waited for him on his desk. Wonderful sensation, that of being himself after these last nightmarish, topsy-turvy days! Mr. Brown thanked God that his life was back to normal again.

The Purring Countess

During the twenty-five years that he had been a minister of the gospel the Rev. Mr. James Starr had known many people well, in the special, intimate way in which a teacher knows her pupils or a doctor his patients. He had met the wicked, the ignorant, the misguided, the foolish, and the good; but until he became pastor of St. Anne's Episcopal Church he had never met a human being whom he thoroughly disliked.

On the first Sunday morning that he presided over his new congregation Mr. Starr had seen this man's face. It had leaped to his eye as he sat in his great carved chair waiting for the choir to finish the hymn; and it seemed to Mr. Starr that the light, the color, and the music dropped away, and that he and this stranger were left in a soundless solitude, staring into each other's eyes. In that moment such a disgust and loathing rose in Mr. Starr's soul that he had to close his eyes and pray briefly for serenity.

In the later course of his ministerial duties he discovered that the man's name was Hector Jamieson and that he was a doctor of medicine. Dr. Jamieson and his wife lived, childless, in an ornate Victorian house on one of the older streets, where it was permissible that the doctor's office be built on at the back of his residence. Mr. Starr noted, in the course of an evening walk, that the neighborhood was a lonely one, wooded and quiet. The lots were large, and the house nearest to the Jamiesons'—a white plaster mansion with a red tile roof—was vacant and had a For Sale sign displayed at the bottom of the drive-way. And though Dr. Jamieson's shingle hung plainly by his side gate there were no cars parked there, nor any people coming or going. This concurred with the whispers Mr. Starr had heard that Dr. Jamieson's patients were exclusively female and came only late at night.

A minister must not listen to whispered gossip, and Mr. Starr closed his ears to it, but the illogical revulsion toward Dr. Jamieson remained. The man came to church every Sunday, and Mr. Starr found himself preaching too often on such texts as "The wicked flee when no man pursueth" and "Vengeance is mine; I will repay, saith the Lord." He told himself that it was merely Jamieson's face that had turned him against the man. As features went, it was an ordinary face, broad, dark, strong-nosed, a mustache partially concealing the mouth. But, really, it was not a face at all, it was a mask; and the alarming thing was that no lively eyes looked out from behind it. The eyes, too, were part of the mask, remote and expressionless. Dear God, what horrors the man must be concealing, to wear a mask *over* a mask! At this point in his reverie Mr. Starr quickly turned to Corinthians to read about Christian charity, and to ask, humbly, that he be granted more of that virtue.

Mrs. Jamieson, on the other hand, he liked at once. She was a slender, nervous woman with a soft Southern voice, an air of good breeding, and an almost childish desire to please. As teacher of a Sunday school class and an earnest worker in the church, she came often to the rectory for consultation and reassurance. "If I'm a burden to you, Mr. Starr," she said apologetically, "please tell me. I know I should try to be more independent, but making decisions —even little ones—has always terrified me."

"I'd be happy to see you every day, if you care to come that often, Mrs. Jamieson."

Her trouble was, he saw, that she was lonely. Except for the church, she had no social activity. "The doctor's evenings are always full of appointments," she told him, "so we don't entertain and we never go out. When we were first married I used to go by myself, but I don't any more. It's impossible, really, for a wife to have a circle of friends that doesn't include her husband." Not once did she intimate that anything more serious than the length of his office hours kept her husband from entering the social life of the town.

He was meticulously careful not to pry. Much as he yearned to hear every detail about Jamieson—how the man obsessed him!—his conscience forbade his asking Jamieson's wife any questions. However, he could not help noticing that she seemed happiest when she was speaking of her childhood, for at such times her face took on a shy radiance and her restless hands lay quietly in her lap. Her maiden name had been Claiborne and she came of a wealthy Georgia family. Her father was dead, but her mother still lived, alone, in the big white house in Atlanta. "I keep thinking," she said wistfully one bleak February day, "how lovely the old place always looks at this time of year. Heavens, how long it's been since I was there!"

"This is the season for migrating," he said encouragingly.

Her hands flew to their nervous clutching of each other. "I couldn't, really. The doctor hates to be alone in the house and—well, he says it's Mother's place to visit *us*." She averted her face and sighed. "He says that if I go running down there it will look as if I were after her money."

"Nonsense!" said Mr. Starr loudly.

Her smile was grateful. "Well, of course *I* know that Mother wouldn't think any such thing, but the doctor's a proud man and he doesn't want anyone to think he expects favors of them."

Mr. Starr wanted very much to say flatly that that kind of pride was a sin, a setting of oneself above the rest of humanity, but he refrained. Instead he remarked pleasantly that he supposed, things being what they were, that her mother would have to do the visiting, and Mrs. Jamieson said that her mother didn't like to travel and changed the subject to potluck suppers.

In spite of her evasions and her polite reticence, he came to have a pretty good picture of what her life was like and he found it appalling. She was not a militant person, but no one could mistake her goodness. How, then, could she bear to live in that lonely house with the mysterious young women going in and out of the gate at night? And could she continue to exist in a social vacuum without friends or companionship? On the other hand, what else could she do? Her husband was not foolish enough to let her go, even if she wanted to. She provided the smoke screen of respectability, she was the reason he was tolerated at all. To his prayers at night the minister added one for the strengthening of Mrs. Jamieson's immortal soul, that it might live with pitch and not be defiled; and he made a point of passing her house on his walks, like a watchman making his rounds. It served no purpose, but it made him feel better.

Then the Countess Vanelli came to town.

The For Sale sign vanished from the lawn of the white plaster mansion next door to the Jamiesons', and the place blazed with lights until late at night. Temporarily Mr. Starr abandoned his nightly strolls down that street, because he encountered so many of the townspeople walking there to stare at the Countess' lighted windows. Feminine breaths were bated while the Countess settled her household, and the planners of parties suspended operations until it could be determined if the Countess would accept local invitations. Mr. Starr found the fuss understandable and natural, but he reminded his congregation, that first Sunday, that they should not render unto Caesar the things that were God's.

The second Sunday he met the Countess. She came to church dressed in a black suit that made other women's heads snap around smartly, her dark hair was drawn smoothly back under her hat, and she sat, in perfect attention, with her eyes fixed on her prayer book. It was not until after the services, when she stood in front of him at the church door, that Mr. Starr realized that she was a woman of over forty. She said in impeccable English, "Can you come to an early supper this evening, Mr. Starr? I should like to become better acquainted. I understand there is no Mrs. Starr, or my invitation would include her, of course. Will five o'clock suit you? I know you must be back at the church by seven. Good. I'll expect you."

He went for supper, diffidently, expecting stiff formality and perhaps even liveried footmen. Instead he encountered simplicity and enchantment. The countess, now dressed in a simple frock, seemed younger than she had in church and treated him as if he were a member of her own generation, ignoring his white hair and clerical collar. Her manners were so beautiful that one was unaware of manners at all, only of a sense of refreshment and of being at one's best. She led him over the house, pointing out what she had done in the way of décor, and he observed that not once did she look in a mirror. He admired, and tried not to envy, her complete lack of self-consciousness, her tremendous poise.

"It's a very large house for just one woman," he said, following her back to the living room.

"But it's so glorious to have space again. During the war, you see, we were interned in our château in Occupied France and Nazi officers were billeted with us. It was not a large place, and with my husband, my two daughters, five officers, and Anna—you can imagine! I vowed then that never would I live in crowded quarters again, and even Anna agreed with me, thrifty as she is."

"Anna?"

"I suppose I should say she is my housekeeper, but she is much more than that. I am not practical, you know, I was brought up to be useless. Anna is my cook, my manager, my friend, my nurse—everything. And very intelligent. If I had my way she would be sitting here with us, talking, but she has firm ideas about the fitness of things. She will bring in the wine presently, and then you shall meet her."

A large orange cat jumped up on the minister's knee and settled there, purring. "No, don't take him away. I like cats. Did you bring him with you?"

"Yes. He belongs to my older daughter. The girls are just finishing their school in Switzerland and my husband will bring them along with him when he comes, this fall, to open his office in San Francisco."

Mr. Starr felt a distinct bereavement. "Then you will not be staying here permanently."

"No. Just for six months. This is just a little vacation for me. I have traveled so much that I longed to live for a while in a pretty, quiet town. So my husband's agent—the one who found us the house in San Francisco, which will not be ready until autumn—found this place for me. Anna and I love it already."

"Your cat likes it too." He smiled down at the throbbing animal on his knee. "I understand that scientists are not sure of what the purring mechanism is, but this cat has a very good one."

"Oh, I can purr too," said the Countess astonishingly.

She rose from her chair and bent her throat toward his ear. Her lips, her mouth were motionless, but from somewhere inside her issued a genuine purring sound, a note or two higher than the cat's.

The incongruity of it made him laugh. "Amazing!" he said.

"I do it only when I'm very pleased, of course," she said, resuming her chair. "Ah, here is Anna."

Anna was a short sturdy woman with ash-blond braids pinned tightly to her head. She dropped a respectful curtsy and set a glass of pale wine by the minister's hand. "It is very light," she said in a heavy, Germanic accent. "It will not hurt."

The Countess waved a hand toward a large painting that hung above the fireplace. "What do you think of that, Mr. Starr? Give me your honest opinion."

"I know very little about painting. I like the colors. They suit the room."

The Countess looked triumphant. "You see, Anna!"

"I cannot help it," said Anna simply. "Matisse and I will never be friends. Van Gogh, yes. Cézanne, yes. But Matisse, no. I am too old for Matisse."

"Seventy is not too old for Matisse. It is that you are excessively orderly. Everything must be just so, just right, and Matisse did not paint like that."

"I can see why you like him, madam, since excessive order is not one of your faults," said Anna, and both women burst into laughter.

Mr. Starr laughed with them. He sipped his wine and watched the Countess' animated face and talked more than he had in a long while. The only awkward pause came at supper when the Countess spoke of her neighbors.

"This Dr. Jamieson," she said. "What kind of man is he?"

The pastor set his coffee cup down carefully. "I—I don't really know the man. He comes to church every Sunday morning and shakes hands with me when he leaves." He hoped that neither his face nor his voice was betraying what an ordeal that handshake was for him, though his conscience would not let him avoid it. "I've never said two words to him, otherwise."

"He's an unfriendly man, I believe. Quite different from his wife."

His face brightened, eloquently. "Yes, Mrs. Jamieson is most pleasant. I'm glad you've met her."

"I ran over there one night to ask for help with our stove. Anna has not cooked with electricity before. Mrs. Jamieson came back with me and was most helpful."

"You'll be good for her. She's so much alone. I hope you can be friends."

"We are friends. She comes every day now, but we have to be careful. Her husband does not approve."

"Why should he object?" said Mr. Starr indignantly.

"Exactly what Anna and I have been wondering," said the Countess. "I thought perhaps you could tell us."

"I'm sorry," he said lamely. "I can't." He was uncomfortably aware that, to so clever a woman as the Countess, his refusal to speak was quite as revealing as anything he might have said.

"The man has a bad aura," said the Countess. "You do

not believe in bad or good auras, I suppose. Too spiritual-istic for your cloth. But I smell malice in the wind that blows off Dr. Jamieson. I shall keep an eye on him."

Mr. Starr went away feeling remarkably relieved, for no reason that he cared to explain to himself; and later in the week, when he saw Mrs. Jamieson as she was about to enter the Ladies' Auxiliary meeting, his admiration for the Countess increased. Mrs. Jamieson was radiant. Her eyes had luster, her cheeks were pink. She laughed on the slightest provocation. Even her clothes were different, in some mysterious way.

"That's a charming dress," he said, smiling.

"Oh, thank you. It's one I've had for some time, really, but the Countess said it needed a touch of color, so I— imagine *your* noticing." He remarked that he was not as eyeless in Gaza as some people thought, and she smiled and went on talking about the Countess. "So many clever people are interested only in themselves, but she takes a real interest in everyone around her. Too much interest, Anna says. Anna scolds her for it."

"Considering that Anna appears to have devoted her whole life to another person, her argument loses force."

"She doesn't know how *good* it is to have someone interested in you," she said gratefully. "I had forgotten just how good it was."

To Mr. Starr, it was equally good to find people who were interesting. Always, when he called on the Countess, there was something that amazed or gratified him. If it was not the sight of the dignified Anna roaring down the drive toward the supermarket on a big, shiny motorcycle ("She learned to ride one during the war," said the

Countess, "and the motorcycle was simpler to transport than a car. I take taxicabs, myself") it was the knowledge that he was the only man who was admitted to the house.

"It would not be proper for Madam to receive even married men accompanied by their wives, since her husband is not in residence," Anna explained to him. "One's priest, of course, is considered an intimate friend of the whole family."

In time he became accustomed to these smaller surprises. But he never lost his astonishment over the conversations he had with the Countess.

Theology, for example, turned out to be a subject on which they were poles apart. Mr. Starr advocated the encouragement of the good which he felt lay in every soul; the Countess was all for the prompt suppression or extermination of the wicked. With approval, she recounted tales of the sudden deaths of Nazi officers at the hands of the citizens in whose houses they were quartered: tales of mysterious food poisonings, disappearances, cars that had been tampered with, a fatal fall down a flight of steps. Mr. Starr hid his shock and reproved her for too flamboyant an imagination.

"The authorities believed that those deaths were from natural or explicable causes," he scolded. "You have no grounds for thinking otherwise."

She retrenched, but only to a point. "I'm certain about the fall down the steps," she said stubbornly. "Those stairs were *waxed!*"

He sighed. "Good housekeepers have a wonderful affinity for wax, I've noticed. I can't believe it to be a murderous tendency."

The Countess looked amused. "My dear Mr. Starr, being a man, you don't know that the one place in a house that is never waxed is the staircase. The stupidest of maids would not do such a thing. Much less a fine housekeeper like Mrs. Schweitzer."

He opened his mouth to say that no fall is necessarily fatal and that Mrs. Schweitzer would not have run such a tremendous risk. But a sudden picture came to him of a man sprawled at the foot of a staircase while a vague figure beat on his head with some heavy object, inflicting injuries that would also be blamed on the fall, and he decided to abandon the argument.

No matter what the subject, however, the Countess managed to startle him. About Mrs. Jamieson she said, "She is too good. A fine woman, but handicapped by goodness."

He nearly leaped from his chair. "How can goodness be a handicap! Am I devoting my life, then, to crippling people?"

Her smile was meek, demure. "What I mean is that, when a good person has to deal with a bad one, the bad one always wins. You have observed that?" He said that he had observed no such thing, but she had returned to the subject of Mrs. Jamieson. "Her husband doesn't even support her, did you know? She has an allowance from her mother. A small one, but still an allowance."

"Perhaps if she had had children—" he began.

"Oh, but the doctor doesn't want children. She told me. At least, he doesn't want them *now* and hasn't for the past fifteen years, but she's sure that he'll want them someday." She threw out her expressive hands. "You see? Faith, loyalty, she has all the virtues. And all they bring her is misery."

"She's looking far from miserable these days," he said defiantly.

"A temporary happiness, built on sand," sighed the Countess. "It cannot last, under the circumstances. You'll see."

He did see. Mrs. Jamieson's contentment lasted through Lent, but when she called at the rectory on Good Friday morning the bloom had vanished. Thin and haggard, all her pretty animation gone, she stared at him with desolate eyes.

"I came to tell you that we won't be able to make our usual Easter contribution this year, Mr. Starr. My husband has had reverses—the stock market—"

He did his best to console her. "Many people are having to retrench, and your past generosity—"

She was not listening. "It meant a great deal to me," she said in a flat, strained voice. "I—I can't tell you how I feel." She had gone before he could say another word.

On Easter morning Dr. Jamieson sat alone in his pew. "She's ill," thought the minister and, for once, was eager to talk to the man after service.

"Sally went to Georgia yesterday," said Dr. Jamieson impassively. "Don't know how long she'll be gone. Her mother's very ill."

"I'm sorry to hear that."

"Mrs. Claiborne's over seventy. Can't expect too much."

"I suppose you're going down later in the week?"

"No. Far too busy. Have no intention of traipsing off to Georgia, no matter what happens."

Mr. Starr took this to be an idiotic pose of some kind, but he was mistaken. Three days later the town buzzed with the news that Mrs. Claiborne was dead and that Dr. Jamieson was not stirring a step to be with his wife in her hour of trial. Nor did he answer his doorbell, though the minister rang several times and was positive that he heard movement within.

Feeling ineffectual, Mr. Starr went to consult the Countess. "I hesitate to impose myself where I'm not wanted. At the same time I don't want to fail in my duty. The man comes to church, he is one of our members—"

"Sheer façade," sniffed the Countess. "He won't let you in because the house probably shows traces of the things that have been going on there. The cheap women. The drinking. When his wife was home there was nothing like that. Oh, he's being subtle about it, but I am not easy to fool. Your Dr. Jamieson has one fault which clever, cold men often have: he thinks other people are much stupider than they are."

Uneasily, Mr. Starr avoided a discussion of Dr. Jamieson's new shortcomings and stuck to the problem. "He must know that his not going to the funeral will cause talk, a thing he has always shunned. Up to now."

"Mrs. Claiborne is dead," said the Countess simply. "She hated him, wouldn't allow him to set foot in her house. But as long as she was alive he had to behave himself a little, because there was always the disposition of her money to consider. Now he can do as he pleases."

"Surely that depends on Mrs. Claiborne's will. A woman of her means must have left one."

"Yes. We were talking about inheritances one afternoon

and Sally told me about it." Mrs. Jamieson was to get everything, but with provisions. The house in Georgia was hers, only if she would live in it. The capital was to remain untouched for ten years, although she was to receive the interest, a considerable sum. "Poor Mrs. Claiborne," said the Countess soberly. "She tried so hard to outwit her son-in-law that she didn't see the terrible thing she was bringing on her daughter."

Mr. Starr was confused. "But he can't touch the money. He doesn't get any of it."

Her voice was softly emphatic. "If his wife dies, he does."

He began to laugh, he couldn't help it. "That imagination of yours! For a nice woman, you have the strangest—"

"You can laugh if you like," she said indulgently. "I hope, when he tries to kill her, that I am still here. I may be able to prevent him."

"You're letting your dislike of the man—which I confess I share—run away with you. How do you conceive these nightmares!"

"I once lived in a nightmare, Mr. Starr. So I recognize one when I see it." She went on, without a change of tone, to say that her garden was full of daffodils and that, when they bloomed, she would give an outdoor tea party in their honor. Watching her count a guest list on her fingers, he felt like the lenient father of a complicated child.

"I'm afraid your party will have to get along without me. Chances are I'll be away, at the District Conference." He explained to her that the Conference was really a week of meetings, attended by all clergymen of a certain denomination, and that, this year, it was being held two hundred miles away. "I've been asked to make one of the speeches, and I must get busy and prepare it."

"It will be the very best speech of the whole Conference," she said with open affection.

Her confidence was warming, but when he began work on it the speech went badly. He struggled with it mightily and Mrs. Jamieson, walking into his study one evening, made a pleasant interruption. He shook her hand cordially and said that it was good to have her back.

There was a new composure and decisiveness about her. She laid a check on his desk, without fluttering. "It's my Easter tithe. I can afford it now." She spoke of moving to Georgia in September. "Seeing the place again made me realize how much I love it. The lawyers have given me six months in which to take up residence. The doctor can settle his affairs here by then." Yes, her husband had agreed that the move was right, much as he disliked country living. "It's quite unselfish of him. Perhaps he sensed that I intended to be firm about it." She pulled on her gloves, thoughtfully. "The Countess was right all along. She says that a doormat is made to be stepped on. I am no longer a doormat."

The transformation in her pleased him so much that he entitled his new speech "Personal Dimensions" and was congratulated, on its delivery, by no less a personage than the bishop himself. Mr. Starr returned home more by cloud of glory than by train. It was nine at night when he reached his station and observed, for the first time, that it was raining.

Fantastically, Anna was waiting for him, under a black umbrella. "Please, Mr. Starr, Madam must see you at once.

I have a cab waiting." Her manner alarmed him, but all he could get out of her was that Mrs. Jamieson was very ill. "We must not talk about it here," she said, nodding at the cab driver's back. "Wait."

The melodrama of the situation infected him, against his better judgment. He nearly ran from the cab to the Countess' front door. She opened it promptly and drew him inside with hands that were like ice. "Thank God you've come. I wanted to send you a telegram, days ago, but Anna wouldn't let me."

"Is Mrs. Jamieson dead?"

"Not yet. Very ill, I think. Virus pneumonia, her husband says. He won't let me see her. He says it's contagious and he's nursing her himself." She began to pace the floor, kicking back the train of her tea gown each time she turned. "No one can see her! She's completely at the mercy of that man."

"Has he called in another doctor?"

The Countess stopped short. "He's poisoning her! Would he call in another doctor?"

"I have tried to reason with you about these nervous obsessions of yours," he said sternly, "but now I am telling you flatly that it is wrong and dangerous to make accusations without evidence. You might be sued for slander, for defamation of character—"

She was not listening. "It must be poison, it has to be. Arsenic, I think. The symptoms are alike—vomiting, pain, irritations of the organs—you must go to the police! At once!"

"On a mere suspicion, not even my own?" He mopped his face with his handkerchief. "It would be scandalous!

A clergyman is the last person in the world to bring unfounded charges."

"Then," she said despairingly, "I must stand here and let the poor soul die?"

Mistaken though she was, her earnestness moved him. "I think I can make Dr. Jamieson see that it would be wiser to take her to a hospital, if she's as ill as you say."

She almost pounced on him. "Yes! Yes! But give him an alternative. Talk hospital, strongly. Then let up a bit and leave the rest to me. Where is my cape? Anna, you come with us."

Afterward Mr. Starr was never sure what had happened. He remembered the march of the small procession through the rain; the grudging way Dr. Jamieson opened the door and the dismay on his face when the Countess swept past him and into the house; the interview, with the four of them standing in the dusty living room; the hatred in Dr. Jamieson's eyes, while his lips strove to be civil. He did not like the mention of the word "hospital," and he liked it less each time Mr. Starr said it. He was quite capable of handling the situation alone, he had given up his office hours to nurse his wife through this thing.

As friends and neighbors, they could not permit such unnecessary self-sacrifice on his part. They were concerned for his welfare, as well as his wife's, and he needed a helping hand whether he knew it or not. Since he did not like the idea of removing his wife to a hospital, some other way to lighten his burden must be found.

The Countess provided the solution. "The least we can do is to take the housekeeping off your hands. I shall lend you Anna. About everything but housework she is very stupid, but she will do for that."

Dr. Jamieson was ready to make any small concession that would get rid of them. "That's very kind of you. If your Anna will come for a couple of hours a day—"

"No, no," cried the Countess. "She will live here until Mrs. Jamieson recovers. I will bring her things over in the morning." Before he could protest she gathered her sable cape about her and moved to the door. "Let her sleep in your wife's room tonight, so you can get some rest. Good night, Anna. Take good care of our neighbors."

The moment they were outside again, she became slightly hysterical, laughing and crying softly as she walked along through the rain. "Your face when I said that Anna was stupid! It nearly gave everything away. But I had to make him think that she would observe nothing that—You are too honest a man to make a good actor."

"I wasn't acting," he said severely, "and there was no reason for Anna to be stupid or to be left there at all, as far as I can see. The hospital was the best idea, but you interfered before I had brought him around to it."

She wiped the tears from her eyes and her voice was faintly exasperated. "What could the hospital have done for her?"

"Made her well, of course."

"And then?"

"Then she could come home."

"And then?"

"I don't know what then," he said irritably, "and neither does anybody else."

She stopped in the reflection of her own house lights and studied him, very seriously. "I do not agree with you that, if you ignore evil, it will go away. But I admire you for always believing the best about people. I think this is a habit of yours by now, you cannot change it if you try. Always you believe the best. Anyone who knows you can count on that."

The open praise embarrassed him. "You're shivering. Better get to bed." She turned obediently to the door, and he risked a little joke at her former fears. "No more visions of Dr. Jamieson sprinkling powders on his wife's food. I need some sleep myself."

"I am not worried any more," she said seriously. "My mind is quite at rest."

He looked back once as he trudged down the drive. She was standing by her fireplace, the cape still about her, looking down at the heavy poker, which she held in her hands. He thought it probable that she didn't know what to do with the thing, and the picture of her tackling the fire, inexpertly but fiercely, amused him all the way home.

He was exceptionally busy the next day. A hundred duties carried him all over town, and it was seven o'clock when, still supperless, he returned to the rectory. By then the message was two hours old. Dr. Jamieson had met with a fatal accident, a fall, and Mr. Starr was to come at once.

The door was opened for him by Sergeant Mayburn, whom he knew well from their mutual work on juvenile delinquency cases. The coroner had come and gone, the body had been removed, and Mrs. Jamieson had been given a sedative by Dr. Powers of the Mercy Clinic.

"Anna and the Countess are upstairs looking after her,"

said the sergeant. "I didn't like to leave them all alone after a shock like that, so I was holding the fort till you showed up."

"I'll telephone some of my church women to come and relieve them. They've done their part."

"Phone's in the hall, at the foot of the stairs." He led the way, skirting an area where the rug was damp. "That isn't blood or anything. It's soap and water. The Countess scrubbed it herself, the minute we said she could. Imagine, a real countess down on her hands and knees with a scrub bucket! The boys was dumfounded. But she had to call Anna to make coffee for us. Can you imagine a woman not knowing how to make coffee?"

Mr. Starr was looking at the stairs, a disturbing memory nudging his mind. Hadn't he heard somewhere about an accident similar to this? But that other fall had been occasioned by waxed treads, while here a neat strip of green carpet ascended the middle, leaving four inches of bare wood on each side. "Is this where it happened?"

"Yep. The carpet's perfect, you can see. So we figure that he stumbled over his own feet and took a header, or that he stepped on that polished wood on the side and slipped. Crashed down into this marble table here—there was blood all over one corner of it—and brought that big brass lamp and all right down on top of himself. Died almost immediately. Head injuries."

The minister bent to run a finger over the shining wood of the steps. It was smooth as glass, but, of course, the carpeting made it reasonably safe. If the carpeting had been there at the time. The idle viciousness of this thought made Mr. Starr jump as if he had been stuck with a pin.

"Clean, aren't they?" the Sergeant was saying. "Anna's work. You know how German women are. You could eat off the floor anywhere."

Mr. Starr's self-discipline asserted itself. He was not going to be guilty of the kind of wicked imagination he had deplored in the Countess. With an effort, he cleared his mind of memory and conjecture alike and resumed his proper duties as a man of God. "I'd better make my telephone calls," he said briskly.

"And I'll mosey along. Police department as small as ours, we always have plenty to do. If we'd been bigger, we might have nailed Jamieson years ago. Never could get the goods on him." He jerked a thumb toward the ceiling. "A nice woman like Mrs. Jamieson. She's better off this way."

Mr. Starr went up the stairs carefully, holding onto the railing. In the doorway of the sickroom he paused, listening to a soft, throbbing noise that filled the air. Mrs. Jamieson, terribly emaciated, lay asleep on her immaculate pillows, Anna dozed in a corner chair, the Countess sat, upright and watchful, by the bed. Her back was toward him, but he identified the sound, even so. Unbelievably, the Countess was purring!

Mrs. Jamieson must be better, then. He stepped forward to inquire and to offer his sympathy.

A Matter of Record

For ten years Josiah Palmer had counted himself fortunate in being principal of Richmeadows High School. Because Richmeadows was a town heavy with wealth and privilege, the high school was an architectural marvel of light and air, the teachers both inspired and conscientious, the classroom loads light enough to permit individual pupil instruction. Mr. Palmer appreciated these blessings, though after Mr. Ogden Sims came into his life he was apt to count them through gritted teeth, as Martin Luther might have told a rosary.

By the time the ruddy, hefty, and terribly vigorous Mr. Sims first brought his son Lawrence to the high school the boy had already attended two private schools.

"A terrible mistake!" boomed Mr. Sims. "Told my wife so at the time. The boy ought to learn to rub elbows with all kinds."

"Unfortunately," said Mr. Palmer, "our own student group is not as diversified as I should like, but—"

"But you don't discriminate, that's the thing! Those other places, if the boy's father was a millionaire, the kid got all A's. Now I'm not a poor man, but I'm not living off my interest yet, either. I'm production manager at Lathrop's, put in a good day's work every day. So the marks they gave *my* kid—well, look at that transcript!"

Mr. Palmer had been looking. The highest grade on the page was an unsatisfactory D in English, and the quantity of red ink expended on failing E's was sufficient to notate a large war map.

"Hotbeds of favoritism," said Mr. Sims. "Lawrence tried to tell me so, and I didn't believe him. But you can see for yourself, they didn't teach him a thing. Didn't try to."

Mr. Palmer moistened his lips. "Do you intend to go on to college, Lawrence?"

"Yes, sir. I'd like to be a doctor, sir."

Mr. Palmer's amazed eyes flew back to the bleeding transcript, and Mr. Sims said approvingly, "Always wanted a professional man in the family. Lawrence ought to do well at medicine. Has the looks and manner for it."

"Looks and manner are all very well," said Mr. Palmer bravely. "There's considerably more to being a doctor than that."

"But nothing that good schools can't teach him, eh? Didn't have a chance to go beyond the eighth grade myself. Not ashamed of it. Had to make a living."

Mr. Palmer hated intellectual snobbery almost as much as he hated ignorance, and he wanted to make that plain. "Many of our finest men have been self-educated," he said quickly.

"Well, a lot easier to let the schools do it for you." Mr. Sims smiled firmly, like a man who has just paid for something and doesn't mean to be fobbed off on its delivery.

"I have every confidence in you, Mr. Palmer. You can count on my full co-operation every step of the way." He left the office briskly, to the accompaniment of the janglings of various small ornaments which sat on the bookshelves.

Mr. Palmer blinked at the boy Lawrence and was unhappy. The youngster had the very virtues that would make his faults hard to deal with. Good-looking, mannerly, eyes alert, he gave an impression of eager normality that belied his past scholastic record. Mr. Palmer, however, knew the two private schools in question and preferred to believe them. Patiently he unsnarled the transcript of credits and gave the boy the benefit of the doubt by enrolling him as a tenth-grade student. "Of course you'll have to take ninth-grade biology over again, since you failed it and it's a premedical requirement. In Latin, our Mr. Hillberry will give you special help in coming up to class standard. And English—well, you'd better enter our remedial English class until you're able to take a regular course."

"Will I get credit for this remedial thing?"

"Oh yes. Yes. It's for pupils who have—missed out—on spelling and composition work. They proceed, each at his own pace, to try to catch up."

The boy grinned. "I'm not much of a speller."

"Ah. There is a literature section to the course also. Do you—ah—like to read?"

"Reading's okay. I'm no bookworm though."

"I gathered that," said Mr. Palmer, writing an extra study hall into the program.

Three weeks later Mrs. Thibaum walked into the principal's office, smiling faintly. "Lawrence Sims," she said simply. "I don't know what to do about him."

Mrs. Thibaum was one of the best teachers Mr. Palmer had, which was why she had been assigned to the chore of teaching remedial English. This admission—equivalent to an experienced general's acknowledgment that he did not know how to draw up a battle plan—was inexpressibly shocking.

"If he's been rude to you—"

"Heavens, no. It's much more serious than that." She drew a paper from her portfolio. "I'd like you to read this. It's a representative sample of his composition work."

Mr. Palmer read:

William Sharespeare was born from 1564 to 1616. His father was a framer, but his mother was related to Queen Elizbean which it is said they is the reason of her son bein so great. Sharespeare marred Ann Hathaway and had two childern. The frist was a son, the second was twins. Sharespeare wrote many plays Macbeth and one they was about a dream. In Macbeth Macbeth and Banquo when sporting by the way togeather.

"Atrocious," said Mr. Palmer. "Make him do it over."

"I make him do everything over, but it isn't going to help. He's the sort who can write 'first' correctly twenty times in his notebook and then spell it 'frist' the next time he uses the word. No carry-over between practice and performance. None at all."

"Have we an I.Q. on him?"

"Yes. It's above average. He's quite capable of good

solid work. He simply doesn't feel responsible for doing it."

"Lazy?"

"Heavens, no. He's a whirlwind of activity. Hurries into class, opens his book, writes furiously, looks at me with luminous attention whenever I speak. But nothing comes of it. I've had several private talks with him about his work, and he just smiles and says, 'I guess I'm quite a problem, all right.'"

"At least he seems to be facing fact."

Mrs. Thibaum put the paper back into her portfolio. "I don't think 'facing' is quite the word. He *acknowledges* the fact. Like people who say, 'Yes, I know I'm fifty pounds overweight,' and then go right on *being* fifty pounds overweight. There's a personal conviction missing."

Just before the mid-term marking, Mr. Palmer made a hasty check of Lawrence's performance in his other classes and found a grievous unanimity of teacher opinion. Mr. Hillberry said that it was almost impossible to teach a foreign language to a student so ignorant of his mother tongue. "The boy doesn't *remember* anything. If *agricola* is a noun today, Lawrence won't recognize it as a noun tomorrow. He retains no vocabulary whatsoever. And this whole business of case—well, if he doesn't know a subject from an object, and he doesn't, how is he going to know what case to use?" Mr. Duncan, the biology teacher, was resigned, rather than aroused. "The boy's an indifferent student, all right. Doesn't belong in a college preparatory course at all. I don't expect initiative except of my very best pupils, but Lawrence can't even follow a simple set of directions. I stand over him and tell him what to do next, though it's all written out on his experiment sheet. Spoon-feeding, but the class is small and I have the time to do it. How he'll come out on the tests is another matter. I can't very well help him there." In accordance with the school policy of giving a new pupil a long time to settle down, they were more lenient in grading than in their private opinions. Lawrence's mid-semester marks were C's (meaning class average) and D's (not satisfactory, but giving hope of not failing).

The report cards went home on a Friday, and Mr. Sims appeared in Mr. Palmer's office Monday morning. His manner was still cordial, but there was a guardedness about it similar to that of a man who suspects he is being cheated in a poker game but is not ready to bring open charges.

"I think you've done quite well for a beginning," he said. "I dare say that, now the get-acquainted period is over, his teachers will be more exact in their estimates of Lawrence's work."

Mr. Palmer's tall thin body stiffened. "I believe they are quite exact now. Your son has had a good deal of their individual attention."

"One can't expect miracles," said Mr. Sims magnanimously. "They have so many students that they have to divide their efforts at first. Now that they know where the difficulties are, they'll have no trouble eliminating them."

Mr. Palmer felt himself growing angry. "You speak as if the matter was entirely up to the teachers, Mr. Sims.

They *have* pointed out Lawrence's difficulties to him. It is now up to *him* to make the corrections."

"I see," said Mr. Sims sneeringly. "Teaching must be a very easy profession. The student does all the work."

For a moment Mr. Palmer could not believe his ears. Then he said, "Of course. We can no more do a student's work for him than we can eat his meals for him."

"A very comfortable point of view."

"It isn't a matter of point of view," said Mr. Palmer, feeling as if he were trying to explain analytical geometry to a three-year-old. "It's a fact! In your business, have *you* found a way of making a man work if he doesn't want to?"

"But Lawrence *does* want to work," said Mr. Sims triumphantly. "He'll tell you so himself. He does every blessed thing his teachers ask him to do! Why, the other day I even caught him reading Shakespeare, and he seemed to be enjoying it, too."

"Sharespeare," said Mr. Palmer.

"What—"

"That's what he called him in a composition. Share-speare."

Mr. Sims laughed. "That's a good one! I'll have to kid him about that."

His amusement was genuine. Mr. Palmer's anger ebbed into helplessness. "But doesn't it seem to you that he *should* have spelled it correctly? After he'd seen it in his book every day and on the blackboard and—"

"I'll tell you, Palmer. Spelling isn't as important as it used to be. Larry, now, he'll have a secretary to do his letters for him and she'll take care of things like spelling and punctuation. Hardly any use his wasting his time on it." He dropped his confidential air and pointed a finger sternly. "Mind you, I'm not telling this to the boy. No, sir. I'm co-operating with you people a hundred per cent. I was just giving you my private opinion."

As time went on Mr. Palmer was to become privy to other opinions that left him reeling. A foreign language, according to Mr. Sims, was a waste of time, unless you got some fun out of saying that you had taken it. "Everything worthwhile has been translated into English. English is the big language in the world today. Any foreigner who knows which side his bread is buttered on can speak English." (But Lawrence, a native, could not speak English, or read and write it, either.) History, said Mr. Sims, was a complete waste of time. "It's water over the dam. Important thing is to know what's happening *now*." (He did not reveal how one might judge the present without understanding the past.) It was his belief that the schools should stop teaching a lot of silly, impractical subjects and concentrate on the things a pupil would be *using* in later life. (By what method a youngster would determine just what he would be finding useful ten or twenty years into the future, Mr. Sims did not say.)

The first year Mr. Palmer struggled mightily to right Mr. Sim's educational theories. He tried to point out that the mind was not departmentalized, that all learning was interrelated. For instance public speaking (a course of which Mr. Sims approved) was impossible without a knowledge of English grammar and a bowing acquaintance with literature and history, for reference purposes.

Not to mention sufficient information on one's subject, the ability to speak being useless unless one had something to say. Mr. Sims contended that all he wanted Larry to get out of a public speaking course was an ability to think on his feet. Mr. Palmer answered that a school merely provided the tools necessary to thinking; it did not and could not teach anyone to think. Mr. Sims said that that was the trouble with schools, right there.

At the end of the first semester, when it was revealed that the biology teacher had flunked Larry (that was the way that Mr. Sims put the fact that Larry had failed once more to learn anything about biology), Mr. Sims decided that his son, obstructed as he was by the teachers of the premedical subjects, should change his course. Mr. Palmer had a fleeting gleam of hope.

"That's very sensible, Mr. Sims. I'm certain that Lawrence would do better in what we call a general course. Shop, mechanical drawing, no foreign language, no history—"

Mr. Sims pondered. "Sounds all right. Can he get into college on a course like that?"

"Well, no. But since it begins to appear that he is not college material—"

Mr. Sims smote the desk. "He *is* college material. Don't go blaming the boy just because your teachers don't choose to exert themselves! Do you realize that a young man can hardly get a job these days without a college diploma? What are you trying to do to the kid, ruin his whole life?"

"That is not our purpose," said Mr. Palmer, his tongue

stiff with rage. "If it seems to you that that is what we are doing, then I suggest that you enroll your son in a different school."

"They're all alike," said Mr. Sims gloomily. "They turn out a bunch of kids that don't know anything, and they're full of holy excuses for it. Why, if I ran my business like that—Do you know that I can't hire a secretary who can spell or punctuate?"

"You had better find one," said Mr. Palmer. "For when Lawrence gets into business, you know." (He rebuked himself immediately for the malicious triumph behind this remark. It was highly unprofessional.)

Mr. Sims appeared not to have heard. "Big shortage of engineers these days. Change Lawrence into whatever will let him take engineering in college."

"But that means mathematics," said Mr. Palmer incredulously.

Mr. Sims looked truculent. "What of it?"

"Algebra. Geometry. They call for hours of hard, painstaking work. I—"

"Let me tell you something, Palmer. That boy *already* puts in hours of work. Sits up in his room for three hours every night, books open all over the place. And he comes to school every single, blessed day. Hasn't missed one!" He rose, like a prosecuting attorney who has just disclosed evidence fatal to the defendant. "Now don't tell me mathematics can't be taught to a boy like that."

"Mathematics can be taught, to be sure. But it also has to be learned."

"Gibberish," said Mr. Sims.

Six weeks later Mr. Downs, who taught beginners' algebra, sought an interview with Mr. Palmer. Mr. Downs was a forceful, brilliant young man, teaching by day and taking his law degree at night school, and he came straight to the point. "Lawrence Sims ought to drop algebra," he said. "He can never hope to pass it, and he might as well be taking something where he has a prayer. For example, I give him a problem: $X + 4 = 12$. His answer: $X = 16$. 'Does $16 + 4 = 12$?' I ask him. 'No,' he says. 'Then your answer is wrong, isn't it?' He guesses so, but he doesn't know why. 'I get mixed up on those plus and minus marks,' he says. 'Never mind the plus and minus marks right now,' I say. 'Use your head. *What* plus four equals twelve?' He pretends to think a minute. 'Oh, I see how it goes now,' he says. But he still can't tell me the answer. 'Eight,' I tell him. 'Eight plus four equals twelve.' He bites his lips. 'But so does six plus six,' he says. About that time I give up."

"His father is determined that he should take algebra. There is nothing I can do. Have you met Mr. Sims?"

"I've heard of him," said Mr. Downs significantly. "Well, if he won't let the boy drop it, I'd better be able to show why he failed. I'll hang onto all the papers Lawrence does in class—no use hanging onto his homework, he copies that from somebody—and when Mr. Sims comes over breathing fire, refer him to me. I'll prove the case so thoroughly that even he won't be able to doubt it."

Oh, wonderful Mr. Downs! In later years he became chief corporation council for one of America's biggest industries, but Mr. Palmer never admired him more than on the June day when he reduced Mr. Sims to the admission that Lawrence did not have the mental equipment for algebra. "Evidently calls for a special talent," mumbled Mr. Sims.

"It calls for study," said Mr. Downs pointedly.

Mr. Sims looked at Mr. Palmer with hatred. "The boy hasn't been taught to study. His teachers haven't seen fit to show him how to do it."

Mr. Downs looked as incredulous as if his face had been slapped, and Mr. Palmer intervened quickly. "Since we are agreed that Lawrence does not know how to study, wouldn't it be sensible to take him out of college preparatory work, where study is so essential? In our General Course, for instance, most of the work is done in the classroom, and—"

"Shop and mechanical drawing!" said Mr. Sims scornfully. "If you can see Larry as a shop man, it's pretty clear that you haven't paid any attention to him. He doesn't *look* like a shop man."

Mr. Palmer forbore to mention the examples he knew of boys who, knowing their families could not send them to college, had taken the General Course and had later worked themselves up to high administrative brackets. He had a notion that Mr. Sims would regard this as a guarantee. "That leaves only the Commercial Department," he said regretfully. "Typing. Shorthand. Bookkeeping. With Larry's English difficulties, I'm afraid—"

Mr. Sims brightened. "Say, that's not such a bad idea. I was reading just the other day that one of the quickest ways for a young fellow to get along was to become some big shot's secretary. You learn to handle a lot of the business for your boss, and pretty soon you've got a good job of your own. We'll start Lawrence in the commercial work this fall!"

He went away in high spirits, and Mr. Downs grinned at his principal. "I'll tell you one word the boss had better not dictate to Larry. 'Algebra.' At the end of twenty weeks he was still spelling it 'alegbra.' "

"Don't blame yourself too much, Harold. He went to Serbrook Naval Academy for a whole year and Mrs. Thibaum showed me a paper he'd written about it. Referred to it as a 'navel' academy, all the way through."

"Makes it sound like a Buddhist monastery, doesn't he?"

After the first card-marking in the fall, Mr. Palmer braced himself for the customary interview with Lawrence's father, but Mr. Sims did not appear. The second marking period came and went, and still no Mr. Sims. Mr. Palmer made a point of seeing Lawrence in the corridor and inquiring as to his father's health. Mr. Sims, it appeared, had never been better. Mr. Palmer returned to his office in a puzzled but beatific state of mind. The relief was wonderful.

The beautitude lasted until March. It was ruined by little Miss Carroll, the typing teacher, coming in to announce, with the ferocity of a white mouse whose maze has been changed, that she was going to be very rude to Mr. Sims, good school public relations notwithstanding. "At first he came only once a month, and I was sorry for him. You know, the way you are with people whose children aren't doing very well. I explained that Lawrence had all the mechanical facility of a good typist, but that he was so ignorant of the English language that it was very difficult for him even to copy it correctly. We agreed that Lawrence would have to sacrifice speed for accuracy, and I was to give him extra copy work, rather than dictation. It didn't work out, though, because Lawrence loves to rattle things off quickly—he really has a very good speed rating, if one mistake every two words didn't count —and he just won't slow down. Mr. Sims started coming around once a week—to my apartment, mind you—and he's getting more unpleasant all the time. Now he says that, since I'm a typing teacher, I should mark only on typing, and not on English. He says that, considering the number of words a minute Lawrence can type, he should be getting an A in typing. And then he gets angry and says unkind, personal things—"

Mr. Palmer's shocked mental processes concentrated on the possible dimensions of the opened abyss. "Has Mr. Sims been calling on Lawrence's other teachers at their homes?"

"I believe he has. It's an insulting business from first to last. He gets to talking quite loud and the neighbors have complained. They—they're putting a wrong construction on his visits. It's all most embarrassing for me."

"You will not be troubled again," said Mr. Palmer grimly, pushing the button for his secretary.

He dictated a concise, dignified letter to Mr. Sims, saying that it was against all scholastic ethics for parents to harry teachers in their private domains. Hereafter, if Mr. Sims wished to confer with a teacher, Mr. Palmer would be obliged if he would undertake the conference at the school and in Mr. Palmer's presence. "As principal, I am responsible to both parent and teacher. Interviews, without my permission and knowledge, are not official, according to state law. If you persist in your present course of conduct I shall have no alternative but to insist that Lawrence leave our school."

Three days later he received Mr. Sims' answer in the mail.

Dear Mr. Palmer:

Your attitude seems very unreasonable to me, but I suppose I must abide by it. Believe me, I would have removed my son from your school long ago if there had been any better place to send him. The whole system of education in this country is so rotten that I might as well put up with the situation as it is. At least I can keep things under observation, much as you seem to resent it. If you would keep your teachers properly on their toes, busy men like myself would not have to try to do it for you.

Since Lawrence will be a senior next year, his grades are very important to me. I have many friends in industry who will be glad to give him a job, and the better his record the better the job will be. I dare say that this is a matter of no interest to you, but I think it should be, and I warn you that I shall continue to be intolerant of the lax attitude of you and your faculty toward educating the boy.

Very truly yours,

Ogden Sims

Intolerance at a distance, thought Mr. Palmer above his anger, was better than intolerance close at hand. He suppressed a strong desire to answer the unjust letter (it was as impossible to answer as if it had been written in Swahili) and took to having bad, tormented dreams at night in which he tried to come to someone's rescue with only a kiddiecar as a means of locomotion, or, threatened, was unable to break through a tremendous hedge to safety. In this ominous outward serenity the school year marched to its close.

Usually Mr. Palmer spent the long summer vacation in reading and gardening and dutifully drinking the milk shakes with which his wife sought to overcome his spareness. This peace and quiet constituted a sort of reverse hibernation during which he stored up the necessary nervous energy for the next school year. But now he found himself restless, irritable, unable to relax. A sense of foreboding hung over him, and he avoided his neighbors, his mail, the telephone, even the evening paper (for any of these might bring in the bad news which, he felt, was sure to come). Two sunny months went by and he could not rid himself of the impression that he was walking down a pleasant road that had, somewhere, been secretly planted with land mines.

The first week in August, just as he was beginning to believe that he was succumbing to delusions of persecution and incipient paranoia, his wife came home from a bridge game and in five sentences convinced him that he was most wretchedly sane. "I met a strange little woman this afternoon," she said. "They'd asked her to fill in. A Mrs. Sims. Her husband's just been appointed to the vacancy on the City Council. If he's as mousy as his wife, he won't be much good."

"Ogden Sims? On the City Council!"

"Oh, you know him. His wife said he went to a good

deal of trouble to swing the appointment. Thought it was his duty. She says he's terribly interested in civic matters. Especially schools."

"How long ago was he appointed?"

"Let's see. She mentioned that he'd been to two meetings and they meet once a week, don't they?"

Mr. Palmer saw disaster and saw it whole. He sped out of the house and entered the adjoining back yard, where Kenneth Cross was tending zinnias. Mr. Cross was head of a large advertising agency, a friend of the Palmers, and president of the Richmeadows School Board. In his profession he was accustomed to handling people who had been driven to dementia, and he had developed the voice and manner of an intelligent angel.

"Well, Jo," he said quietly, but somehow achieving the effect of a fanfare of welcoming trumpets. "Where have *you* been all summer?"

"I came over to tell you that the School Board's in for the worst kind of trouble," Mr. Palmer blurted, finding it difficult to move the great blocks of rage out of the path of communication.

Mr. Cross transferred his thoughtful gaze from the zinnias to his visitor. "The School Board's always in trouble," he said mildly. "What have we done now?"

Mr. Palmer poured forth the saga of Mr. Sims. "The only reason he wanted to get on the Council is so he could throw mud at the high school, discredit us. He'll use any method, any criminal falsehood. I tell you, we have to *do* something!"

"Let's sit down and talk this over, Jo." Mr. Cross led the way to a garden seat and took out his pipe. "Now. What purpose could Sims have in wanting to discredit the school?"

"Don't you see? So when his son's deplorable record has to be shown to somebody Mr. Sims can say, 'Poor Lawrence went to that crazy school you've read about in the papers. Naturally he wasn't very popular there.' He's about to throw a whole school system into the fire, just to make one boy look better! That's exactly what he's going to do. I *know*."

"You're absolutely right, Jo." (Mr. Cross had the habit of using frequently the first name of the person to whom he was speaking. To the emotionally lost, this had the reassuring sound of a father calling to a strayed, frightened child.) "I wish I'd known this sooner. I'd have dealt with Sims a bit differently."

"He's already begun?"

"Yes. Oh yes." Factually and calmly Mr. Cross recounted the main points of the Sims campaign so far. Mr. Sims, it appeared, wanted a loyalty investigation of every teacher, especially history teachers. ("That would be Miss Bates and Mr. O'Brien. Miss Bates is a firm Catholic, and O'Brien was a major in army intelligence up to three years ago.") Mr. Sims was demanding that all teachers live within the city limits. ("I told him that some of our best teachers were married to men who had to live near their work and that, frankly, most teachers couldn't afford to buy the expensive houses we have here. And *he* said that teachers were public servants and should be easily available to the community at all times. He sounded as if he might recommend building a barracks for them.") Mr. Sims was going to make it his personal business to discover why students could go through Richmeadows High School without being taught anything. ("I explained to him that eighty per cent of our students learned quite a bit, while the other twenty per cent got by on a very low grade of performance. Unfortunately all our diplomas look alike, so that a prospective employer can't tell a thing until he sees the student's transcript. I asked Mr. Sims whether he advised our making a distinction at commencement time—giving diplomas to some and mere certificates of attendance to others, but he didn't want that either. Said it would be an easy out for the schools, wouldn't it?")

"You see, I've been thinking of the guy as honest but misled," Mr. Cross finished. "Now that I know it's pure malice—"

"It has to be balked. What can we—"

"Well, we can't suppress him," said Mr. Cross reasonably. "All we can do is try to answer him."

"You *can't* answer him. He's immovably ignorant. He doesn't want to be informed. All he wants is his own way."

Mr. Cross drew reflectively on his pipe. "You're sure that all that has him on the warpath is his son's poor marks?"

"People whose children get good marks don't complain about schools," said Mr. Palmer simply.

Mr. Cross smiled slowly and beautifully. "Jo!" he said. "Good boy! That's the answer!"

"I—what answer?"

"People whose children get good marks don't complain about schools," said Mr. Cross significantly.

"But that's no—" The outrageous implication struck him. "Look here, we can't do a thing like that. Even if we wanted to, we couldn't."

"Why not?"

"It—it would be unfair to the boy."

"Would the boy think so?" asked Mr. Cross gently.

"No. He'd be delighted, but that—"

"And the father?" persisted Mr. Cross. "Would *he* think it was unfair to the boy?"

"No, but his shortsightedness doesn't release the school from its obligation to—"

"This is no time for nobility, Jo. With our whole school system in danger of being unfairly publicized and slandered?"

Mr. Palmer stopped gasping and thought, and the longer he thought the more glorious the wicked scheme appeared. He began to feel happy and refreshed. He slapped Mr. Cross on the back. "It'll serve the old boy right!" he cried.

"I'd take it as a great personal favor," said Mr. Cross humbly.

"First day of school I'll talk to Lawrence's teachers."

"In strictest confidence."

"There'll be only five who have to know, and some of them have been through the fire already. They'll co-operate."

"If there are kickbacks of any kind, you can refer them to me, Jo."

"I'll deal with them myself!" said Mr. Palmer, his own man again.

The second day of school Mr. Palmer issued certain

instructions to five members of his faculty, who accepted them with the amused awe of people about to perpetrate a shocking but very funny practical joke. A month later he held a brief conference with Mr. Cross over the back hedge.

"I notice that the *Town Crier* is no longer giving its front page to Mr. Sims and the school system," he said cautiously.

"He's calmed down a good bit, Jo. Oh, he still growls a little whenever he sees me, but his heart isn't in it. Yesterday he told me that Lawrence had made an A on a typing test."

"Don't you think he'll suspect? He's not a stupid man, you know. Willfully ignorant, but not stupid. Won't it strike him as flagrantly improbable that—"

"If I know Sims, he's not the type to suspect good fortune. Don't you go getting nervous about it. I tell you, we've cut the ground right out from under his feet!"

Report cards went home the middle of October, and two nights later Mr. Cross came over and did a tap dance on Mr. Palmer's kitchen floor. "I've just come from the big bridge party at the club—must have been three hundred people there. Sims made an opportunity to speak to every one of 'em. Wanted them to know that his son had all A's on his report card. We're a success, Jo! He loves us!"

Mr. Palmer's inconvenient conscience gave him a twinge. "I—I feel a little sorry for him, in a way. It's natural for a parent to be proud of—"

"Wait till you hear! When he got to me with the news I said, 'The high school seems to have improved since I last talked to you.' And he said—get this, Jo— 'I guess they know now which side their bread's buttered on.'"

"He didn't!"

"Yes, he did. So, you see, he isn't a bit worried about the marks being bona fide, just as long as Lawrence *gets* them."

"What an abysmally shortsighted man," said Mr. Palmer sadly.

"And terribly bad at public relations," said Mr. Cross gleefully. "Offended three hundred people at one crack! Doesn't know that nothing disheartens a parent so much as hearing that somebody else's kid is getting wonderful marks. Why, when my boy George made Phi Beta Kappa up at State, I told Carol that if she breathed a word about it I'd divorce her. Wait and see. Within a month Ogden Sims won't have a friend in the world!"

But at the end of the first term, when Mr. Sims came to call on the principal with Lawrence's report card, a solid blaze of A's, in his hand, he seemed to be in high good humor. By pretending to upset his inkwell, Mr. Palmer managed to avoid shaking hands (this would have been the act of a kissing Judas) and said an extra-cordial good morning to make up for the omission.

Mr. Sims came right to the point. "Thought it was only fair to come over and tell you how pleased I am, Palmer." He laid the report card on the desk and pointed to it. "Wonderful! Keep it up!"

"Well, I—it's the teachers who give the marks. I have nothing to do with it, really." Mr. Palmer's humility was beautiful to see.

Mr. Sims winked. "Oh, I imagine you have a *little* something to do with it. Keep it up, that's all I want to say. Two good friends of mine have already offered Lawrence jobs after he graduates. They're important men and he can take his choice between them." He tapped the card with his finger. "All on the strength of this."

Mr. Palmer cleared his throat. "Secretarial work?"

"Yes. Secretary to the boss, either way. That is, if his record this next semester is as good as his last."

"Have you any reason to think it won't be? I'm a little confused as to—"

Mr. Sims scowled. "I don't intend to get into a discussion about it. All I came to say was that there'll be no complaints if you keep on exactly the way you're going!"

But there were complaints. Mr. Tyson (the study hall supervisor and not one of the Informed Five) came in a few weeks later to say that he was having to deal with a student insurrection that centered about Lawrence Sims. "I have him in two study hall periods and the same thing happens both places. When I assigned seats for the new semester—four to a library table—nobody wanted to sit at the same table with Lawrence. It surprised me because I hadn't known the boy was unpopular, before."

"I don't think he was—before. What did you do?"

"I made the three others I had assigned to the table stay there. We don't seat study halls by popularity or unpopularity, I told them." Mr. Tyson took out a handkerchief and wiped his palms. "Perhaps I should have let them change. They're making quite a point of being rude to Lawrence. Don't look at him, won't speak to him—"

"Well, it's only for the rest of this year, and since there are only three students who—"

"It's *not* only three of them. The whole study hall got into it. You know how we allow the superior students to give a little help to the ordinary ones? Well, pretty soon, one at a time, half the study hall was going to Lawrence to ask him questions about their lessons. They did it quietly and I didn't object, but I couldn't help seeing that bad feelings were building up. He didn't know the answers—or wouldn't give them—and they'd sneer and walk away. Yesterday Peter Fairchild went over to him, and the first thing I knew"—Mr. Tyson applied the handkerchief to his forehead—"Pete had hauled Lawrence out of his chair and was yelling at him, 'How come you get A's if you don't know anything, you big, stupid ox!'"

"Good heavens," said Mr. Palmer uneasily.

"For a minute it looked like the French Revolution. I have a hundred and fifty youngsters in there and they were muttering and snarling and telling Pete to let Lawrence have it! I managed to calm them down and I had a little talk with Pete afterward—he's a good boy, just lost his head for a minute—but what will happen today I don't know. The situation's pretty tense."

"I will allow Lawrence to drop both study periods," said Mr. Palmer promptly. "Will you find him and tell him so?"

"But—but that's no solution, is it, sir? Wouldn't it be better—I don't mean to criticize—to try to straighten out the situation, rather than to dodge it? After all, our students have to learn not to resent achievement. Isn't this—"

"Ordinarily I'd agree with you," said Mr. Palmer, "but I rather think this is a special case. We will drop Lawrence from the study hall rolls."

A Matter of Record

Despite his outward firmness, Mr. Palmer was shaken. Where there was so much student dissatisfaction there was bound to be parental disturbance too. He kept a cautious ear tuned to the humming of the community grapevine and was relieved when all it brought him was a vague, discontented opinion that Mr. Sims was, somehow, "putting one over on the school." Not one parent came to the school to question or blame. Mr. Palmer reflected that there was nothing so conducive to getting away with murder as having led a long and honest life up to the point of the crime. His digestive processes, however, demanded something in lieu of good conscience and he was obliged to soothe his stomach with soda tablets, before and after meals.

Lawrence Sims himself precipitated the crisis. With the first week of April, he began to be sporadically absent from school, missing some twelve days out of a possible twenty. The attendance officer investigated and brought his report to the principal.

"He's been truant, all right," the attendance officer said. "His mother thought he was in school right along. It's his *reason* for cutting that's brand new to me. He says he's stayed out of school because he doesn't want to get all A's any more!"

"Unbelievable, isn't it?" said Mr. Palmer.

"Seems the kid's slated for some wonderful job or other, with a friend of the family's, and every time this friend sees one of the boy's report cards he makes the job even bigger. Throws in more things for Lawrence to take charge of, till the kid's scared to death. 'Well, scared or not scared,' I told him, 'the state law says you have to be in school every day unless you have a valid excuse for being out. And with all this absence,' I said, 'you won't have to worry about all A's on *this* card-marking!' "

"As a matter of fact, his marks did not go down."

The attendance man whistled. "You mean that he did twenty days' work in five? He must be a real world-beater!"

"It would seem so," said Mr. Palmer, playing with the bottle of soda tablets that stood on his desk.

The second week in May, Lawrence was absent again, three days in a row. On the fourth, shortly after school had been dismissed for the day, Mr. Sims walked into Mr. Palmer's office. His gait was slow, like a sleepwalker's, and his voice was muted. Upon invitation, he sat down heavily in the visitor's chair and stared out of the open windows into the quiet street. Mr. Palmer had to ask him twice, gently, why he had come.

"Larry's marks," said Mr. Sims almost inaudibly. "They'll have to be changed."

"I'm afraid that isn't possible," said Mr. Palmer truthfully. "Once a mark has been given it must stand."

Mr. Sims sighed. "Well, I don't know. It—it begins to appear as if you people have—overestimated the boy."

"Our estimates are sometimes wrong. But, after all, it's what a student really knows that counts, not what the teacher *thinks* he knows. All marks are relative."

"The point is that Larry feels that such a *good* record will be a handicap to him when he applies for a job. He—he feels he can't live up to it."

Sympathy and guilt warred in Mr. Palmer's mind. He

148

spoke earnestly and consolingly. "The handicap will be temporary, surely. However we rate him, the truth will out."

"He asked me to test him myself, and today I did," said Mr. Sims with a touch of his old defiance. "Those marks *must* be removed. They're ridiculous!"

"I'm sorry. There is nothing I can do."

For a moment he was afraid that Mr. Sims might explode into honesty, shouting that he was the victim of a put-up job and had no intention of standing for it. But, to do that, Mr. Sims would have to admit that he had once been very, very wrong, an admission that was entirely out of character and equivalent to a confession that he had learned a lesson. Mr. Palmer waited.

"In that case," said Mr. Sims bitterly, "I had better take Lawrence out of school entirely."

"You can do that, of course. He's more than sixteen."

"What will that do to his transcript—record—whatever you call the damned thing?"

"When we send a transcript to an outsider we use only the final marks for each semester. If Lawrence leaves school now, all his subjects this semester will be marked simply Incomplete."

Mr. Sims brightened. "Then, counting the whole four years, that leaves only one batch of A's out against him?"

"If you want to put it that way. Yes."

Mr. Sims rose. "Drop him at once. It'll solve the problem."

"I'll take care of it immediately."

Mr. Sims rose and held out his hand. "Thanks," he said.

Mr. Palmer shook hands cordially and saw him to the door. Then he threw the bottle of soda tablets into the wastebasket and went home to enjoy his dinner for the first time in a year.

In Name Only

Norma Corcoran walked briskly and lightly down the aisles of the department store, nodding to the salesgirls, straightening a trinket on a counter, indicating stock that should be folded and put away. She liked making this ten o'clock tour of the store. As head of personnel she checked on the appearance of her girls as well as on their sales slips. At Klinger's, hair must be neat, dresses immaculate, blouses not too sheer, scent not too strong. And she felt that it did the girls good to see that she herself was abiding by the rules she had made. Her chestnut hair was rolled neatly on her tall head. Her dress was a simple black that had cost forty-five dollars even with her store discount. It made her look slender and pleasantly sedate.

Not that she expected her clerks to pay forty-five dollars for their dresses. No one knew better than she that they couldn't afford it, for she had been one of them until two years ago. Then she had been working in a Klinger's store back in her home town in Iowa and, by the time she had grudgingly spent enough to keep herself looking respectable, there had been precious little to take home to help her parents. But she had been ambitious. Now, at twenty-five, she was in charge of all the hiring and firing here, and there had been rumors that the national executives had their eyes on her, that if she did well here she would be transferred to a branch in one of the larger cities. It was those rumors that kept her working at her desk long after hours, that kept her isolated from the life of the town. She was bounded by the store, the library, various restaurants, and her splendid room at the Richardsons'.

It worried her mother. The letters from home were always saying, "Don't work so hard, honey. Enjoy your youth while you have it." Norma could never convince her that the feeling of getting ahead was all the fun she needed. That, and the pleasure of being able to send gifts that made life more comfortable back home. An automatic washer. A power saw. An electric mixer. A pretty hat, bought with her store discount.

The handkerchief counter was crowded with women drawn by that day's special markdown and the salesgirl had the frantic look that betokened inaccurate sales slips and confused service. Norma stepped behind the display cases and reached for a pad.

"Who was next?" she asked.

As she drew out handkerchiefs for inspection and slipped them into green paper bags she became aware of a conversation between two well-dressed women who were waiting their turn. A name they mentioned reached out and caught her ear. Mark Matthews. A pretty name, an interesting name. Mark Matthews. It developed that Mark had a wife named Rosemary.

"And I guess that's the last time they'll ever be asked anywhere. People are fond of Mark but they're not going to put up with her a minute longer!"

"I tried to get Ann to tell me what happened, but she wouldn't."

"Well, there were four tables of bridge and everything went nicely. Ann always does it up brown, you know. And then we went into the dining room and had something to eat and the evening was sort of tapering off. So Rosemary says she's ready to go home and runs out and gets her hat and coat. Mark gets up too, but people keep talking to him and maybe it's ten minutes before he gets out to the hall where she is. I was right behind him, so I saw everything that happened. 'Ready, sweetheart?' he says to her. She didn't look any grimmer than she usually does, but she reached up and slapped his face—you could hear it all over the house—and then she marched out without a word to anyone!"

"And left him standing there? In front of all those people? What did he—"

"There wasn't much he *could* do. He told Ann that he didn't think Rosemary was feeling well and that he was sorry, and he left. You know how nice he always is."

"Why does he stand for it? He ought to leave her!"

"Of course, but there are the kids, you know."

Poor Mark Matthews. On the way back to her office Norma slipped into the accounts department and pulled out his file. Mr. Matthews was thirty-five years old. He owned a house in one of the better suburbs. Ten years ago he had bought largely and paid promptly. But in the last seven years the charge had dwindled and even that modest sum would come in as much as three months late. "Good but slow" was the notation at the bottom of the card. That was strange. As a research chemist for Davis Oil, he should be making enough to meet his obligations. Poor management. His wife's fault, probably.

She slipped the file back guiltily, reproaching herself for her curiosity. But the name stuck in her mind.

It was inevitable that she should meet the townspeople sooner or later. Mrs. Richardson, her landlady, had reared two daughters of her own and she could not stand the sight of a personable young woman working till all hours and then coming home to stay in her room. She introduced Norma to a Mrs. Hanlon and Mrs. Hanlon invited Norma to a beach party.

"It won't be anything to write home about, Miss Corcoran. Just a wiener roast down at the beach. First week in May—we ought to have some nice weather for it, don't you think? My kid brother Red will be down from the university that weekend and I just have to find somebody near his own age for him to talk to. So I thought that perhaps you'd put up with a bunch of old fogies for an evening in a good cause."

"I'd love to come."

And so it was that, sitting in the shadows between a beach fire and a new moon, knowing Red was admiring the chestnut fall of her loosened hair, she first saw Mark Matthews.

"And where Sis dug you up," Red was saying, "is beyond me. I thought I knew everybody in town. Everybody young, anyway."

"Your sister can't be much more than thirty. I'm not so much younger."

"Why, you're a child. A gorgeous moonlit child."

On that precise cue she noticed the man who was moving at random through the changing, milling group on the other side of the fire. He was a very handsome man, tall and rangy, with waving brown hair and a gentle mouth. He seemed to be a great favorite. Men dropped an arm on his shoulders when he passed and women sidled up to him like purring kittens. His quick blue eyes were friendly and his smile was frequent, but there was a loneliness, an aloofness about him that reached out and touched her heart. "Who's that man?" she asked Red.

"The tall one? That's Mark Matthews. He's a good egg with a terrible wife. They don't go many places because nobody can stand her. I guess Sis took a chance that she'd behave herself tonight."

As casually as that, the card in the file had become a person, a body attached itself to a name, and her long curiosity was slaked. Somehow it was embarrassing, disturbing. Embarrassing because she felt as though she had been reading his private mail. Disturbing because—well, she couldn't watch the play of firelight on his handsome face calmly. Really, she must be turning foolish!

"Which one is his wife?"

"There she is, putting wood on the fire."

"Why, she's pretty."

"Pretty enough. But see those two deep lines between her eyebrows? They're permanent and they didn't come from smiling."

"Is it because she's jealous of him?"

"I don't think so. Not especially. It's just any old thing she can lay her tongue to. Hey, they're starting to roast the hot dogs. I'll bring you yours."

He scrambled away and Mark's shadow fell across her. "Hello," he said.

She sat up quickly, shyly. "I know you're Mr. Matthews. My name is—"

"Norma Corcoran. I've inquired."

He was only being kind. There was no reason for her to feel like a schoolgirl!

"It's a lovely evening, isn't it?" she said.

He sat down companionably. "Don't feel that you have to talk to me," he said. "Personally, I don't mind a little quiet. Lots of confusion at home, you know. Two young boys racing around and—well, Rosemary is an angel, but she is talkative."

"How old are your boys?"

"One's seven and one's five. Now I've given myself away as a dull old family man and I didn't mean to. I should have said, 'Lonesome, girlie?' and patted your shoulder."

She laughed. "I really think it's better this way."

Red came panting up with wieners and buns and Rosemary was right behind him.

"Well, darling," she said to Mark, "I see that you've found someone to fetch and carry for you." She turned to Norma. "I think Mark's beaten even his own record tonight. He hasn't done a single thing except talk to people and enjoy himself. No nasty helping to build a fire. No tedious whittling. No—"

Mark's voice was low but there was passionate entreaty in it. "Rosemary, please!"

Norma leaped into the embarrassing breach.

"He was telling me about your two sons, Mrs. Matthews. He sounds very proud of them."

"He should be even prouder of himself. In all the years they've been alive Mark's managed never to be ten minutes alone with either one of them. Still, you adore children, don't you, darling?"

Mark said miserably, "I like children. Yes."

"And there's nothing you wouldn't do for them, is there? Like mending their toys or—"

"You know that you mend the toys before I—For heaven's sake, Rosemary, let's not air our troubles in public like this. I've asked you and asked you to—"

Bert Hanlon strolled over. "My wife wants you to help her with the coffee, Rosemary. Sit still, Norma. It's Rosemary I was sent to get."

Rosemary said bitterly, "A man with a mission," but she went. Red mumbled something and disappeared. Norma and Mark were left in a circle of wretched silence.

"I'm sorry," he said. "Sooner or later I'm always saying that. She's pleasant enough with everyone else, you know. But there's something about me that seems to drive her insane."

"I don't know what it would be," she said.

"Sometimes I think it's because I have more fun than she does. I enjoy life more and people get along with me. It makes her hate me, almost." He put his head down on his arms and his voice was muffled. "It's all right, except that I don't know what to do about it. I honestly don't know."

"Don't let it spoil things for you. Anybody can see that it isn't your fault."

They were calling to him, they were coming over to get him. "Mark, get your banjo. We want to sing!"

He tried to protest but they pulled him to his feet. He shook them off for a minute. "I'm the only man alive in this generation who still plays the banjo," he said. "Good night, my dear, and thank you very much."

Rosemary's voice came clear and sharp across the firelight. "He's been sitting on his hands for so long that they're asleep. If you can make him sing for his supper, it'll be more than I've ever been able to do."

Bert Hanlon said, "Oh, shut up, Rosemary," and his wife laid a quick hand on his arm.

They pulled him into the center of the circle and thrust the glittering banjo into his hands. He smiled at them while his fingers strummed tentative introductions and she heard his baritone beginning a familiar song. The other voices rose raggedly around his. The gallantry of him made her want to cry.

"Take me home, Red," she said. "I don't feel very well. I have to go home."

Her pretty room with its french doors opening on an unsteady upper porch had always before had the power to soothe, to console her. But now the soft gray rug, the chintz draperies she had made herself, the puffy blue lounge chair had lost their potency. The only thing she saw was Mark's face with its patient smile. All she heard was his voice saying, "Good night, my dear. Thank you."

She couldn't go on thinking about him like this. It was wrong and silly and fruitless. She would write a letter to her mother. That would calm her.

She suspended her pen over the writing pad, but the words would not come. She wanted to say, "Dear Mother, I have fallen in love with a married man who is everything that is fine and charming and whose wife makes his life a hell." But Mother wouldn't understand a thing like that. How could she, when Norma didn't understand it herself? She put the pen and paper away.

For more than a year she did not see Mark again and during that time she grew restless but her bridge game improved vastly. She was trying to make a small slam at Ann Milligan's one night when she first heard the great news about him.

"Saw Rosemary on the street today," Sis Hanlon said, "and I asked her right out. She said the decree ought to be final within a month. She gets the youngsters."

"And the house?"

"No. He keeps that. And he doesn't have to pay her any alimony. Isn't it funny that she's divorcing him instead of the other way round? I suppose he let it go that way so it would look better for her."

"What grounds—or didn't she say?"

"Oh, incompatibility or mental cruelty or one of those things. Norma, if you'd finessed the clubs you wouldn't have gone down."

"I know. I guess I just wasn't thinking."

"Three down. My fault for chattering like that. There's something about being dummy that makes me burst into oratory."

Ann Milligan said, "Well, we'll just have to find some-one else for Mark. Somebody nice this time."

"That'll be a job! Everybody's married except the hope-lessly homely."

"Norma isn't."

"Why, sure enough. And she'd be perfect for him! Why didn't I—"

Over the rapid pounding in her throat she tried to quench their enthusiasm. "Listen, the poor man's seen me only once, and anyway, Rosemary's probably cured him of women for good. Don't—"

"We'll have to arrange something. I'm giving my Christ-mas open house in two months. I'll ask Mark and then Norma will be the extra girl for him."

Still she discovered him first by herself. She walked into Blazeby's Restaurant one evening for her dinner and he was sitting alone at a table, staring out at the cold autumn rain outside the window. He looked tired, his suit was out of press, there was a droop to his shoulders. But when he turned and saw her his smile was as warmly magic as ever.

"The gods are kind, Miss Corcoran. Sit down and let me order for you."

They sat in their tiny rose-lighted booth and he talked and talked, as a man does who has been quiet too long.

"When I went to the university the old College Inn was still standing and I used to eat there. This place is a lot like it. Funny that I haven't seen you here before."

"It's tiresome eating in the same place every night. I change off."

"Not much of a business, this living in one room and eating out, is it?"

"Aren't you living at your house?"

"Not right now. It's pretty far out and I hate to drive all that way for—nothing."

"I'm sorry."

"You've heard. Of course; the whole town knows. You don't have to pity me. I'm better off this way. Except that I miss the children. I'm supposed to be allowed to see them whenever I want to. But—I've been only once and I don't think I'll go again." He kept his eyes on his plate. "They didn't want to see me. I suppose their mother's been talking to them, conditioning them against me. They seemed to be glad when I left, and that hurt terribly."

She was indignant. "Really, she should be restrained. I never heard of such a thing. Setting children against their father when—"

"It's all part of that strange bitterness she built up against me. I told you on the beach that night that I'd never understood it. I still don't. But there it is. And now let's talk about something pleasant. Let's talk about you."

By the time he drove her home they were old friends. Yet he did not ask her for a definite time when he might see her again. For several weeks she had to depend on running into him accidentally and, when she did, he always seemed anxious to prolong the occasion but never ready to set a definite date for their next meeting. The suspense kept her tense, irritable. She told herself that she admired him for not getting tangled up with a new woman so soon after his divorce; she rationalized him into being the burnt child and herself the fire. But the persistent casualness of their connection was a blow to her pride.

The social machinery driven by the women she knew began to grind out invitations for the two of them. Presently they were together several nights every week. As a couple they began to be taken for granted. Mark didn't seem to object. Neither did he tell her he found it pleasant. It humiliated her, made her feel silly for caring so much for him. By spring she started refusing the invitations that she knew were to include the two of them. If Mark didn't want her, let him discover someone he *did* want. Pettishly she hoped that he would telephone so that she could be cool to him. He never did.

One sunny Saturday afternoon in May he caught up with her on the street. "Saw you going by the drugstore," he said. "I deserted a perfectly good sandwich for you. I've been thinking I'd take a run out to the house this afternoon. Want to come along?"

Nothing about the three weeks he hadn't seen her. No sign that he had missed her. Here was her chance to show him that she wasn't a girl who could be picked up and put down again.

"I don't believe—" she began stiffly.

His hand was confident on her arm. "The drive would do you good, Norma. Please."

She tried to keep her manner cool but he was at his most captivating. By the time they reached the house his warmth had drawn the pain out of her like a poultice, and when they turned into the driveway and she saw the neglected lawn and the overgrown shrubs she knew that she was too sorry for him ever to be cross again.

He shut off the motor and sat back, his smile gone. "It looks worse than I thought it would," he said. "I'm almost afraid to go inside. It must be a shambles in there."

"Would you rather I stayed out here?"

"No. No. I brought you along to give me moral courage."

He walked her around his half acre first. "Look at the bugs on this evergreen. Probably too late to save it."

As they rounded a corner she had to stop and blink at a tremendous crimson and yellow and purple circle, set like a huge seal in the middle of the back yard. Tulips, hundreds of them, nodded at her.

"I'd like to have a picture of them in color. Mother thinks she has tulips. She should see these!"

"Rosemary planted them two years ago." He was smiling at the tulips and on his face was the same patience she had seen on it first.

"It seems a shame to pull them up," she said tentatively.

He was again brisk, impersonal. "Why, I wouldn't pull them up. Why should I? I think they do the place a lot of good."

They entered the house through the screened porch door.

"There's furniture for this," he said. "Chairs and tables and things. They're stored down in the recreation room. Or I should say in what's going to be a recreation room when I get it finished. I had it nicely under way when I left."

He unlocked the back door and she walked into a small but adequate kitchen.

"Double sink," he said. "Breakfast bar. Electric stove. Linoleum pretty badly worn but that can be replaced."

She laughed. "You sound just like an agent showing a house to a prospective tenant."

He smiled at her. "Maybe I am."

Her heart leaped wildly but she kept her eyes down. She could not believe that he had meant it, but if he had he would have to be more explicit than that. The living room, the dining room, the bedrooms floated past her in a haze. She had an impression of dust everywhere, dented springs in the sofa, worn spots on the rugs and, in the children's room, a dreadful vacuity.

"It's a beautiful house, Mark."

"I think it is. Needs a lot of work. But you don't mind working on a place you own." He took her hand. "How about it, Norma?"

"I don't think I—"

"I'm asking you to marry me. The house is asking you. You can see we both need you."

It was only after he had let her out at her own door and she had rushed, radiant and excited, into Mrs. Richardson's arms to tell her the news, that she remembered that he had not said a word about love.

Their friends were delighted. There were showers for Norma and parties for the two of them. Their days glittered with the golden warmth of the well-wishing for their felicity.

Mark thought she should have an engagement ring. "You ought to have something to show that it's legal," he said. "Let's take a trip to Cleveland and see what we can find."

"I'd rather not. We need so many things for the house, there are so many things I want to do for it. A ring I can only wear on my finger, but a house I can wear all around me."

"But your mother will think I'm a pauper if she comes here for the wedding and sees a shabby house and no ring besides."

"She'll think that I'm eminently sensible. You can give me a ring on our silver anniversary, when the children are all grown up and we're rich."

It was a risk, that reference to children, because she knew that he missed his boys. But she had to let him know that there would be other children and that their love for him would make up for the old loss.

Now he sat silent, twisting a match folder in his fingers, and she hurried on. "It won't take long to get caught up. I make quite a bit of money for a woman and I've saved three or four thousand dollars. That ought to—"

He put an arm around her shoulders and hugged her. "You're sweet, Norma. There are only two things wrong with that. One is that your money isn't leaving the bank. It's yours and it's going to stay that way. The second is that you're not going on working. In spite of the fact that I don't handle it very well, I make quite a bit of money too."

She wailed, "But I can't give up my work! I love it."

"You'll like your new job just as well. And I'm selfish enough to want you all to myself."

His face was so handsome that she knew she couldn't

refuse him. "It can be any way you want it, Mark. If you love me."

"Good girl!"

"You've never said that you love me. You're not saying it now."

He said lightly, "Of course I love you. At first I thought of you just as someone I liked to talk to, someone I could count on to cheer me up. Even that day at the house, I hadn't thought of you as more than that. But all of a sudden, seeing you standing in that kitchen, I knew that you belonged in that house and that I couldn't let you go. You were surprised at my asking you to marry me that day. Well, you weren't any more surprised than I was. It was an impulse and I'm not generally impulsive."

"I hope you haven't regretted it since."

"I'm not much of a hand for regret."

The glittering wheel of the days turned faster and faster. The store gave her a party and a silver coffee service. Mrs. Richardson sent out the wedding invitations. Norma's mother arrived from Iowa and was caught up in the hurly-burly of the wedding preparations.

"Your father couldn't leave the office. He'll come down at the last minute. Where's your young man?"

"Right here. Mother, this is Mark. Please say that you like him."

"I'll wait awhile for that. I will say that he's very good-looking."

"I'll try to be as good as I look, Mrs. Corcoran."

"That would be very good indeed."

But alone with Norma, her mother voiced some qualms.

"I wish his first marriage hadn't been such a failure. It's a bad sign."

"Rosemary was a shrew. She was always after him, nagging and scolding, and he took it better than anyone else would have. Nobody could have lived with her."

"Darling, these things are almost never one-sided. Of course he may be an exception and for your sake I hope he is. But he'll have his faults. Don't you forget it."

"Everybody has faults, Mother."

"Now you're cross with me. Please, dear, I'm only trying to say that an unsuccessful first marriage isn't a good recommendation for a successful second. And besides, you'll be living in a house where his first wife lived and doing and saying the things she did and said, in part, and every now and then you'll wonder about her and—"

Norma laughed. "What you're trying to say is that I'm bound to be jealous of Rosemary. Honestly, I won't. It's just as if she had never been."

"She and the boys still live in town, don't they?"

"Yes, but that doesn't matter. Mark doesn't care about her; he never thinks of her."

"Well, I certainly didn't come here to spoil your wedding and I've done all the crapehanging I'm going to do. Where's that wedding dress you tried to describe to me in the letter?"

There were things you could find out about a man only by being married to him. Within six months Norma had learned two basic lessons: first, that Mark would never get up in the morning without an hour's exhortation on her part; second, that he liked fine things and was a child about money. He refused to let her put their budget on a business basis. She couldn't even discover what his salary was.

"Mark, I'm not trying to pry but I can't tell how much I should spend for groceries or things for the house if I don't know how much we can count on."

"Let's do it this way: you figure out how much you need for food and incidentals every month and I'll give it to you. The rest of the things I'll pay by check when the bills come in."

The first month he gave her the amount she had set, but after that she had to remind him of it.

"I'm going shopping tomorrow and I'll need my house-keeping money, please, kind sir."

"Will ten see you over? I forgot to cash a check today. I'm short of cash."

After that there would be nothing until she asked him again. It irked her to have to do it. The money was for necessities. It wasn't as if she were squandering it on herself. She took to drawing a little bit here and there from her savings account to avoid bothering him. When the bills from the utility companies, the charge accounts, and the home finance office came in, she put them on his desk without opening them. They were not her concern.

The man who came to the door one blustering March afternoon made them her concern. He was a Mr. Hayes from a credit company and he was courteous but firm.

"I'm sorry to intrude like this, Mrs. Matthews, but I am never successful at seeing your husband. I've tried to make appointments with him; I've tried to see him at his work; I've talked to him on the telephone. I don't think he realizes the seriousness of the matter. He borrowed three thousand dollars from us over a year ago and he hasn't given us a cent for ten months. Naturally we're interested in getting our money back, but we don't want any unpleasantness. We don't want to attach his wages unless we have to."

She was frozen with shock. "I—I didn't know he had borrowed anything," she said.

"He said he had a lot of little bills and he wanted to pay them off. Said he'd prefer paying to just one place instead of all the places he owed. Lots of people do that."

She went to her purse and took out her own checkbook. "If you'll tell me the exact amount, I'll write you a check for it on my personal account."

"Thank you, Mrs. Matthews. Thank you very much."

When Mark came home she handed him the receipt with the "paid in full" stamped on it.

"What this?"

"They were going to attach your wages. I paid them."

He exploded. "Do you mean to say they had the nerve to come right out here to the house and bother you? They knew they'd get their money. They didn't have to—"

"I don't know how they'd know they'd get it. For ten months they haven't got anything, not even a chance to talk to you."

"I've had other things on my mind. I don't sit around all day thinking about a bunch of skinflints. There are more important—"

She faced him coldly. "Mark, I have to know the state of our finances. I can't go on blindly like this any longer. If I'd known you owed all that money I wouldn't have bought slip covers and draperies and dishes and heaven knows what all. Now I have only eight hundred dollars of my own left, and if there are any more overdue bills, let's pay them and start fresh."

"There aren't any. I got in over my head last year, I'll admit. Since then I've been going around in a fog. The divorce and meeting you and getting married—don't be angry with me, darling. I'll pay you back, every cent."

She let herself be pulled into the circle of his arms. "You don't need to. I was glad to be able to do it. If you had only let me go on with my job for a little while until we could really straighten things out!"

"It isn't money I need. It's you. You're so sweet, Norma."

"Let's be careful then, shall we? Let's not spend a cent we don't have to."

"Anything you say, sweetheart."

In the fervor of his embrace she believed that he meant it. When, two evenings later, the Hanlons and the Milligans descended on her just before Mark came home, she refused their pleas that she and Mark come along out to dinner at Northern Inn with them.

"Honestly, we couldn't. I have dinner all ready. Why don't you come back here afterward? I'll get hold of another couple and we can have two tables of bridge."

She wished they would hurry and leave. Northern Inn was terribly expensive and affairs like this were Dutch. She wanted to save Mark the embarrassment of having to refuse in person, but he walked right into the midst of them, his words kicking up little gusts of laughter, his smile kindling their gaiety anew.

"Three beautiful women waiting for me to come home!" He turned to the husbands. "Gentlemen, you are excused."

"You ought to be a salesman, Mark. That soft soap would come in real handy."

"Yeah, he's wasted in the job he has. All we came for, you Blarney-stone kisser, is to see whether you two would come out to Northern Inn and have dinner. The good lady can go out and turn off the oven and serve hash tomorrow."

"I'd like to go. Haven't been out there in a long time. Let's have a cocktail first."

Norma followed him out to the kitchen. The noise back in the living room covered their whispers.

"We oughtn't to go, Mark. It'll cost us ten dollars before we get through and we can't afford it."

"Oh, sure we can. It's only once in a blue moon we do anything like this. Have beans the rest of the week to make up for it. Where's the liquor?"

"There's just that little bit. I didn't want to spend the money to—"

"Good night, you have to have liquor in the house! Get some more tomorrow."

"With what?"

His face was patient. "With the money I'll give you if you just have the sense to ask me for it."

"I have asked you for it! I've asked you every month for half a year."

"Lord, Norma, this is no time to quarrel. Save it until they're gone."

That hurt. She felt the tears spring up behind her eyelids and she had to fight to maintain her composure. "I'm trying to be practical."

"Well, whatever it is, take off that cross face and let's get going." He walked into the living room, cocktail shaker flashing in his hands. "Norma can't remember to keep the liquor supply up, but there's enough for one round."

Ann Milligan was observant. "What's wrong, Norma?"

Mark set the shaker down and looked amused. "Norma is happiest when she's saving money. The dinner in the oven will not be eaten. That is not practical. Ergo, Norma is unhappy."

The Hanlons and the Milligans exchanged uncomfortable glances. Sis Hanlon said, "Listen, Norma, if you'd really rather eat here and have us come in for bridge later—"

Mark's betrayal and the unfairness of it had stunned her. Strangled by embarrassment, she sat and stared at her cocktail. Knowing that she must seem sullen and unfriendly, she could think of nothing to say.

Mark's voice was coaxing, the voice of a reasonable man to a difficult wife. "Be a sport, honey, tell them you want to go."

Somewhere she found the strength to down her drink and smile. "I'd like to. I don't know what all the shooting's about."

They all laughed approvingly and Mark said triumphantly, "Atta girl!" as if she had just won a battle over certain hidden but unpleasant tendencies known only to himself.

A blazing anger at him kept her warm and sparkling until midnight, when they were finally alone. Then as she folded bridge tables her rage was a bitter taste in her mouth and she was cold and lonely.

Mark yawned. "Swell evening. Say, do you mind if I

leave all this to you? Have to get up early, but you can sleep. Don't bother with breakfast." She did not answer and he paused with his foot on the bottom step. "What's the matter?"

"I resent being presented as a miser and a wet blanket, that's all. I'm neither one. You know perfectly well that we agreed to—"

"Lord, let's not start an argument now. We'll be up all night!"

He went upstairs and was sound asleep by the time she had washed the coffee cups. She slept in the guest room that night and her dreams were unpleasant.

Her pregnancy occurred just as she was getting ready to ask Klinger's if she could have her job back. It settled decisively the running argument she and Mark had carried on for months.

"You're not going back to work. I won't have you making me look like a fool in front of the whole town. I don't make such a bad salary and I bring home every cent I make. The way you talk, I could be spending it on drinks or women."

It was a well-known fact that he drank very little, that he did not raise an eyebrow at any woman. She was grateful for these things and she preferred not to make an issue out of that "bring home every cent I make."

"You do very well, Mark, but these aren't ordinary times. It takes—"

"If old Linton ever dies or retires, I'll be in charge of the whole lab and then we'll have more money than we know what to do with. Can't you be a little patient?"

She could not make him see her side of it and she was almost ready for open defiance when the doctor's verdict quelled her, gave her absolution, made her happy. For a long time she had worried about Mark's two sons, whom he never saw. He must be lonely for them, though he didn't say so. Once when a group of husky romping boys went by, she thought a shadow crossed his face.

"Why don't you go to see them, Mark? I have their Christmas presents all wrapped and you could take them over."

"You can mail them."

"But it's terrible to have children grow up without ever seeing their father. They—"

"They don't miss me. And I wouldn't want to take the chance of running into Rosemary."

"You're two civilized adults. She wouldn't bite you. Chances are she wouldn't even be there. She's working now that the boys are both in school, Ann told me, and she has a housekeeper."

He frowned behind his newspaper. "Just don't worry about it, Norma. If I prefer not to go, that's my affair."

Once she had said thoughtfully, "You can't hate her that much, a person you'd lived with for ten years."

His face was genuinely surprised. "I don't hate her at all. I just don't think about her."

In her heart she was convinced that he was lying to make her feel better. No one could forget a wife and two children that easily. But now she had something to offer him that would take their place and she could not stop babbling about it.

"Would you rather have a girl or a boy, Mark?"

"I don't care. Girl, I guess."

"You could be more excited."

"I'll wait till it shows up for that."

"Well, you'd better get to work and finish that recreation room. It'll give him a place to play next winter."

"Can I eat dinner before I start?"

She laughed and noticed the unaccustomed relaxation of her face. Perhaps she had been too demanding, too impatient with Mark; too ambitious for him. The baby would take her attention away, make her minimize her husband's shortcomings. The baby would make everything all right.

But as the months dragged on toward spring, the laughter died. For one thing she was overworked. Besides the washing and ironing, cleaning and scrubbing, there were the tremendous dinners Mark insisted on having every evening. Meat, potatoes, a vegetable, a salad, a dessert. Not a bought dessert. One she had made herself.

That winter she cleared miles of snowy walk and driveway with an awkward shovel. The neighbors kept their walks clear; she would have been ashamed to do less, and six inches of snow in the driveway was enough to discourage Mark from even thinking of going to the office.

The most difficult things for her were the handy jobs about which she was completely ignorant but which had to be done nevertheless. The hours she spent on a leaky faucet or a defective wire! And then Mark would discover her work and howl with mirth.

"Well, you're a mighty poor apprentice, sweet. That's a brand-new method. You should have it patented."

"It works."

"You might have asked me to do it. I'm not a bad handyman."

"I did ask you. Four times."

"You have to keep at me, you know that. And as a last resort you could have called Bailey and he'd have come and fixed it."

"I had no money to pay him."

"He'd wait. Not everybody is as strong for cash on the line as you are."

She would not incur bills that might not be paid for a long time. No money. No money. The thought ran through her days like a dirge. Mark demanded that they keep up their social contacts. There would be plenty of time to stay home after the baby came, he said.

"Why don't you go along without me, Mark? All I want to do is go to bed."

"We can't very well hibernate for the next six months."

"Why can't we? The doctor says I should."

"Doctors are all killjoys. Women have babies every day. There's no need to make such a fuss over it."

Ordinarily she set her teeth tightly and went along. This time she stood and looked at him.

"This baby isn't anything special to you, is that it? You've shown me that over and over again. Funny I can't seem to get it through my head. You don't care."

She was docile after that one outburst. She did not mention the baby to him again, even to ask for the money for the layette. Instead she took the major part of her own small hoard to buy all the cheerful appurtenances of a nursery. Often she would go to sit in that small room, folding her hands in her lap, watching the sunlight slip along the walls. A peace came to her there that she could find nowhere else.

The closetful of beautiful expensive clothes she had brought with her when she married was useless to her now. She had to buy two inexpensive maternity dresses and Mark frowned when he saw them.

"They're certainly terrible," he said. "Don't they make any better ones?"

"You can get better ones, but they're expensive, and for clothes I'll use such a little while—"

"That's right. It won't be forever." He reached over to take her hand. "That's one of the things I've always liked about you, honey. You're always so beautifully dressed."

"Good clothes last a long time."

He missed the irony of that. He was engrossed with big plans. "I must begin thinking of something nice to give you when the baby's born. A Mother's Day present, so to speak. How about the diamond ring you wouldn't let me buy before?"

Her chin dropped. She had learned that he was a man who disliked facing reality, but this was fantastic. "For heaven's sake, Mark, think of my hospital expenses! If I could just be sure you'd have enough to take care of those I'd be happy."

He looked complacent. "Maybe I'm better off than you know. Haven't seen any bills coming around lately, have you?"

"No, but I thought you were having them sent to the office or something. I can't imagine that they're all paid."

His laughter was boisterous. "You're a suspicious creature. What've I done that's so terrible, sweet? Don't you love me any more? What's gone wrong? Don't you trust me?"

"How can I trust you when you never do the things you promise? And then manage things so cleverly that everyone thinks it's my fault, that I'm a peculiar person. Your friends think you're married to an ogre."

"Funny little ogre with a nice round tummy."

"I'm serious. I resent being sold down the river just to make you look better."

"You make me sound charming."

"Don't be angry, Mark. If we're going to understand each other, we have to—"

"I'm damned if I understand *you!* Here I ask you if you wouldn't like a nice big diamond ring and all I get for it is some hard words about my general character. If that's—"

Her hands were beginning to shake again. "Are you trying to tell me that you have the money in hand to buy me a ring like that?"

"I'm telling you that I could manage to buy you a ring like that and that it's none of your business how I'd go about it."

Patiently she held him to the point. "Do you have the money right now for it?"

He slammed his newspaper down on his knees. "No, I don't. But there is such a thing as credit, and mine's still good!"

She saw his face mouthing angry words but there was a drumming in her ears and she could not hear him. The walls of the room were flapping like loose canvas and the

178

solid edge of the table slipped away from her fingers. A giant force was pressing her head down into an oblivion where nothing was static, where great currents of darkness surged and ebbed in sickening flux.

When she opened her eyes she was in her own bed and Mark was taking off her shoes.

"Lie still," he said. "I'll make you comfortable and I'll call the doctor. How do you feel?"

"All right. You don't have to call the doctor, really. I think it was just that I had too big a day. I weeded the tulip bed this afternoon and I felt a little funny then."

"I'd have taken care of the tulip bed this Saturday. I told you that. Why on earth couldn't you wait till then?"

Her voice was factual, without rancor. "I've waited for three Saturdays."

"Then it wouldn't have hurt to wait one more. The reason you did it was to make me feel bad."

She said humorlessly, "No, I did it to get the weeds out of the tulip bed."

When she woke it was one o'clock and he was not in bed. The house was very quiet. She put on a robe and went downstairs. The lights were still on and Mark had fallen asleep in the big chair with a newspaper on his lap. In the dining room the dinner dishes sat untouched. It was two o'clock before she gave the last plate a shine and turned out the light on an orderly kitchen. She waked Mark and saw that he got to bed.

In the morning she knew by her sodden pillow that she must have gone on crying in her sleep, so complete was her present despair.

Her mother thought that Terrence was a beautiful baby.

"Looks just like you, Norma, and he's as good as gold."

"I'm so glad I can watch you take care of him for a couple of weeks. I don't know the first thing about babies. He terrifies me."

"It's a big job, but you get used to it. Mark's had some experience. Make him help you till you get back on your feet."

She had been too proud to give her mother the slightest indication that Mark could not be counted on. She said lightly, "I'll do that."

But it was impossible to keep up for long the pretense that her marriage was a success with Mother's keen eyes watching Mark, evaluating him, weighing him and finding that weight short. Much as Norma loved and needed her, she was almost glad to see her go. But she could not keep from crying when the warm familiar arms hugged her in farewell.

The June sunlight made a prism of her tears as she watched the taxi drive away. Still weeping, she stumbled up the stairs to the nursery where Terry was asleep. She wiped her tears away lest they fall on him and leaned over to adjust his blanket tenderly. At that moment he was the only thing in the world that stood between her and total desolation and she was grateful to him for it.

She took care of the baby with the thoroughgoing conscientiousness that had made her a success at Klinger's. Terry was always clean and warm and dry and happy. His meals arrived on the dot. She stole time from the eternal demands of the house to make his outdoor airing hours long, because she loved to see the pinkness of his face in the exhilarating cool weather and the golden tan that sunshine left on his square little shoulders. Nothing was too much trouble for her if it was good for Terry, and she was rewarded by seeing him grow into the biggest, most aware, most amiable two-year-old in the neighborhood.

Mark said she was making a complete fool of herself. "He isn't the only child in the world, you know. You're spoiling him completely."

"He plays for hours by himself now and he gets along well with other children. If I were spoiling him he'd have temper tantrums or refuse his food, and he doesn't do any of those things."

"Other women don't go to all this bother and their kids grow up all right. You're wearing yourself to a shadow and Lord knows you go to bed early enough!"

"I have to get up at six-thirty no matter what day of the week it is, Mark. Unfortunately Terry doesn't know a Sunday morning from a Wednesday. He expects them to be all alike."

"It wouldn't hurt him to stay in an extra hour or two in the mornings."

"No, it wouldn't hurt, but that's not the way to look at it. The point is, would it do him any good?"

Sometimes this bickering over the baby drove her into a flaming temper.

"If you'd ever raised a hand to help with him, I'd think you had a right to criticize. You've never so much as washed his hands. You don't know anything about him and yet you insist on giving me advice out of that vast ignorance of yours. God help the child you had charge of! He'd be fed when you got around to it, he'd spend his whole day in a play pen, he'd go to bed at four in the afternoon and be expected to sleep until ten the next morning. If that's the best you have to offer, just keep quiet."

"You might at least try not to sound like a shrew."

"It's a wonder I don't sound worse!"

She did the best she could. She kept the house and the baby up to the mark, and she let the outside go except for the seasonal demand of struggling with screens and storm windows. The lawn was full of weeds that she had to ignore. When she could spare a dollar she hired one of the neighborhood boys to cut it. Grass usurped the flower borders and insects finished the roses. Even the sturdy tulips had succumbed, throwing out pale infrequent blooms like shadows of their former glory. Looking at them out of the kitchen windows as she washed the dishes, she was surprised by a thought that struck her motionless. Rosemary had managed two children and a tulip bed besides. Rosemary had been a better woman than she.

Mark said that evening, "Guess I'll go down and work on the recreation room after a while."

She heard her own voice screaming, "Don't ever mention that recreation room to me again! I don't want to hear about it!"

As they stood in the quivering silence that the lightning flash of her hysteria had left behind it, the back door opened and Bob Milligan walked in.

"What's wrong?" he said. "Norma see a mouse?"

She dared not risk an answer from the tightness of her throat.

Mark said, "We were just having a little argument. Norma gets excited."

"I'll say she does. I heard that yelp just as I was getting out of the car and I very nearly got back in and drove away. Thought you might have a burglar or something in here, and I'm a timid soul!"

His labored geniality made her smile. "It wasn't as bad as it sounded. I'm sorry."

"Lord, don't mind me. On Ann's nervous days I just get out of the house."

He had come to ask Mark to go bowling with him, if Norma didn't mind.

"Of course if you can't spare him, make like I didn't say anything. Ann's playing bridge tonight and I'm just wandering around getting into people's hair."

She could have kicked Mark for the gentle pleading in his voice. "Could I, Norma? I won't be late."

"It's more than all right with me." Funny how sharp her voice sounded these days, even when she didn't mean it to. She turned a cool cheek to Mark's unexpected good-by kiss and saw that Bob was watching her intently. He was putting two and two together, she could see that, and when he and Mark were by themselves he'd add up and get some kind of answer. Not the right one. Answers like Norma's insane flare of temper when her husband offered her a diamond ring. Mark's engaging social manner in contrast with her own quiet tenseness. Work and don't worry. Live and let live. Let a smile be your umbrella.

To help win back the good opinion of their crowd, she

pretended to be enthusiastic about the yearly October dance at the country club.

"It'll be wonderful to go dancing again. We haven't in so long."

Mark was delighted. "I didn't think you'd want to go. I told Bert I'd have to see."

"Of course we'll go. Except, kind sir, I'll have to have a new dress. I have nothing to wear."

"Now, now. With that boatload of clothes in your closet?"

"Darling, they're almost five years old. Styles change. You don't want me to look like something out of *Godey's Lady's Book*. Anyway, I'm a lot thinner than I used to be. Nothing fits."

"Can't you take 'em in or something? My tux is in rags. Don't know whether we can afford for both of us to be stylish."

She patted him repentantly. "You get the new tux. I'll make out somehow."

She had planned her work so that she could spend the day of the dance making herself pretty, taking in her dress, setting her hair, contriving something that would serve as evening slippers. She went to bed early the night before so that she would be rested and fresh.

At three in the morning she wakened sharply. Terry was calling her and something was wrong with his voice. She ran to the nursery in her bare feet.

The minute she saw him she knew that he was very sick. His little face was red and hot, his hands were restless on the quilt, his breath rattled in his throat.

She wrapped a blanket around him and lifted him into

her arms. She didn't know where to start. You couldn't call a doctor at three in the morning.

She went downstairs, lulling him as best she could, and got out the baby book, running her finger down the list of familiar childhood illnesses. Croup! That's what this sounded like. Half an aspirin and a steam kettle; some grease on his chest. A little ipecac if the phlegm in his throat grew too dense.

By five-thirty he was better. As she sat rigidly in the chair by the crib, she could see that his breathing was easier, that he was more comfortable, knew his temperature had abated somewhat. At seven she went downstairs to call the doctor and make him promise to come out sometime that day.

"You did the right things, Mrs. Matthews, but if it turns out to be more complicated than we think we may have to give him sulfa. Keep him in bed and give him all the liquids he'll take. I'll be out about ten."

She wakened Mark with furious whisperings, admonishing him to dress quietly and not disturb the baby. Back in the kitchen, she could scarcely wait until the coffee was done. She drank it so hot that it scalded her throat.

Mark said that it would be a beautiful evening for the dance. "Usually pours cats and dogs on our gala occasions. Looks as if we'll get a break this time."

She had forgotten that he did not know that Terry was sick. "The doctor can't be sure what it is until he sees him this morning, but whatever it is, it's not good. I'm terribly sorry, Mark. I did want to go."

"He'll be all right by this evening. Kids get well in a hurry. Anyway, he'll be sleeping. He won't miss us."

She tried to be patient. "If he were well I wouldn't mind. But when he's sick—"

He pushed his plate away petulantly. "I knew you'd find a way to get out of going!"

Wearily she tried to be patient. "Isn't there some way you can go by yourself?"

"It's only for couples and you know it! Listen, Mrs. Dunnegan used to be a practical nurse. She can handle him."

"If he wakes up frightened he'll want me. He's too young to take assurance from anyone else."

"I don't know why he should get the decision every time. I want you too!"

Her silence encouraged him. He came round the table to kiss her cheek. "Let's wait and see what the doctor says, shall we? It may not be as bad as you think."

She knew then that she would have to go with him.

The doctor said that Terry was a pretty sick boy. "Picked up a bad bug somewhere, but he's strong. The hard part will be to keep him in bed. Chances are his temperature will go down during the daytime and he'll want to get up and play. Don't let him. Forget about your housework and sit right here and be an entertainment committee. Rest and quiet, those are the main things."

She spent the day between the kitchen and the nursery. While Terry napped, she put her hair up on curlers and prayed that it would dry in time. She gave herself a manicure while she watched him take a wooden toy apart in his crib and she brought her three evening dresses in to brood over them. The white chiffon was the best, though time had turned its color to cream. But she had no slippers to wear with it. As a matter of fact she had only one pair of shoes that were respectable. Fortunately they were black kid pumps and she could get by with them if her dress were not too festive. That ruled out the blue sequined one too.

It would have to be the black. She took off her house dress, slipped the dress over her head, and turned to her mirror with an expectant smile. The smile died and she stood there staring at the impossible reflection. Surely this dress had never fitted her! She took handfuls of the cloth, pulling it snug at the waist, ruining the graceful line of the front drape. It was still hopelessly large. Her eyes traveled up to the bare shoulders of the scarecrow in the mirror and she stood transfixed. Where had all those bones come from, the knobby shoulders, the acute elbows? In the last three years she had had so little time for looking in mirrors. Hurriedly she took the dress off before it made her cry.

She was not very good with a needle. Good enough to take darts and tucks in her street clothes, but not good enough for a job like this. Well, she couldn't be too particular. She would stay in a dim light and be so animated that people would watch her face and forget to look at her dress.

She gave Mark sandwiches for supper. When Mrs. Dunnegan arrived she gave her instructions about the medicine and the steam kettle. Worriedly she hung over the crib, not wanting to leave. Terry was sleeping but his temperature was up again. She could tell by his restlessness, by the ominous thickening of his breath.

"Sure, he's a sick boy, Mrs. Matthews. Anybody with

half an eye can see that. I'll do what I can for him." Her eyes said that his own mother would be better.

"We won't be late. Here's the number of the club. If he gets worse and cries and wants me, don't hesitate to call. I can get back in ten minutes."

She ran into the bedroom to take out the curlers. Her hair was still wet and the curls slipped out lankly. She had to pile it on top of her head to achieve neatness, and the severity of the coiffure was not kind to her thin throat. Rouge and powder helped a little. Her last look at Terry did nothing to reassure her and she went down to the living room with an anxious face. Mark rose from a chair in the splendor of his new dinner jacket.

"I told Mrs. Dunnegan to call the club if he gets worse. Oh, Mark, do we have to go?"

He did not answer and the quiet made her look at him. He was staring at her as she had stared at the mirror that morning.

"Good God, Norma, was that the best you could do? I've never—where did you get that dress? And what have you done to your hair?"

"I did the best I could. It's not very good, I know."

"You look like a refugee. Listen, you've got to do better than that. You must have something else!"

"I could have if I'd had some evening shoes."

"Well, why in the world didn't you get some? Why can't you take care of yourself properly? Other women do. You had plenty of time to order the right shoes. You were just too lazy to do it."

If she cried she'd look even worse. "I didn't have the money to buy new shoes."

"You could have asked me for it. A wife ought to keep up her appearance, do her husband credit. You—"

Rage relaxed her, made her feel warm and alive. "Darling, if I asked you for money every time I needed it I'd be doing nothing else. Because I always have to ask two or three times and then you usually find some good excuse for not giving me any."

"You did this on purpose, then. All I have to say is that it's a lousy time to take to point out a great moral lesson!"

She threw her jacket around her shoulders. "It'll be a great consolation to me during the evening to know that you think I look so well. Are we going or aren't we?"

It was not an auspicious beginning and the evening did not improve as it went along. Mark danced the first dance with her and then was swallowed up by the attentions of the women who declared that it had been ages since they'd seen him, that he and Norma mustn't bury themselves that way. They said this to Mark. They smiled vaguely at Norma and let her alone.

"Don't mind the girls," Bert Hanlon said as he took her into the bar for a drink.

"Just ginger ale, please, Bert. One touch of liquor and I'll fall off this stool."

"That would be no way for a new member to act."

She looked around the snug room, so elegant in its purple plush and flashing chrome. "I'm not a member. We've never joined."

His eyebrows went up. "You are now. I'm treasurer here and I got Mark's fee in the mail last week. Say, maybe I shouldn't have mentioned it. He probably wants to surprise you with it."

Carefully she tucked her inappropriate shoes up on a rung where they would be hidden by her skirt. "How much does it cost to belong?"

"Five hundred dollars is the initial price. After that it's only a hundred dollars a year."

The knowledge lay in her mind like a stone the rest of the evening. Five hundred dollars to belong to a country club, while she pinched and saved and scraped to get by on no money at all! As she danced at the perfunctory invitations of the husbands she knew, as she sat on the edges of sprightly conversations, she studied the gilt cornices of the room, the crystal chandeliers, the expensive draperies across the wide windows. She, Norma, with her old shoes, her ill-fitting dress, and just enough money in her purse to pay Mrs. Dunnegan when she got home, owned part of all this splendor. The inconsistency of it was so great that she could not be angry. On the contrary she felt silly and aimless and hopeless and sad.

It was almost midnight when the page boy brought her the message that she was needed at home and she hurried to find Mark. He was sitting out a dance with the Stanleys' pretty young niece, talking seriously with his head bent while she listened with a gentle sympathetic face. They jumped when Norma touched Mark's arm.

"Will you take me home, Mark? The baby's awake and Mrs. Dunnegan can't do anything with him."

Instantly he was concern. "Of course." He turned gallantly to Miss Stanley. "Good night, my dear, and thank you," he said.

Norma ran to the cloakroom to get her jacket and then stood waiting in the foyer. Her mind churned with her guilt at leaving Terry, tortured itself with pictures of the struggle that was going on at home, heaped reproaches on herself for deserting her duty. Ten minutes! She walked rapidly back to the main ballroom entrance. Across the floor she saw Mark standing in the center of a group of men, laughing, his hands in his pockets, his whole attitude proclaiming that he did not have a care in the world.

It would have been a pleasure to feel her fingernails against his face. Instead she turned and walked rapidly out the front door. The parking-lot attendant brought the car.

Mrs. Dunnegan met her at the door. "Thank God you're here! He won't take his medicine and he's screamed himself hoarse for you. His temperature—"

She lost the rest of it as she flew up the stairs to the nursery. Terry sat in the middle of his crib, a sodden defiant miserable little lump, fighting for his breath. She picked him up and he clung to her trembling.

"Mommy's here, lamb. We'll have you all better in no time. Get the ipecac, Mrs. Dunnegan."

The dark syrup made him retch and she held a basin for him to vomit. She put clean pajamas on him while Mrs. Dunnegan whipped fresh sheets onto his bed and brought in the vaporizer. In half an hour he was asleep, clean and comfortable, his breathing easier.

She gave Mrs. Dunnegan her money and called a taxi for her. "Mr. Matthews was in the middle of a dance and I didn't want to disturb him. You don't mind taking a cab, do you? I'm sorry you had so much trouble."

"Don't give it a thought. When they're that age it's hard to deal with them when they're sick. If I could have managed him at all I'd not have disturbed you." The lights of the taxi came up to the drive and she wrapped her scarf around her head. "I made a pot of coffee while you were busy with him. Chances are he'll be fretful all night long and you'll need it."

She took a cup upstairs with her and sipped it beside Terry's bed.

Every now and then he would waken and she would lean forward so that he could see her plainly. His lips would smile and his eyes would close again. She was not a prayerful woman, but there were prayers in her heart that night.

Mark came home at three o'clock. "I had to wait until someone left, to get a ride. What was the matter with you, running off without a word? I told you I was coming."

"It doesn't matter. I made out all right."

"Good Lord, I came as soon as I could!"

"There are taxis. Or you might have telephoned."

"It's hardly my fault that you insist on acting like a crazy woman, running out like that before I could even get my coat. The whole club was talking about it."

"But you explained my side of it, I'm sure."

"I didn't have to explain anything at all. They know you're unbalanced about that kid and that you don't give a damn about me!"

"And they're sorry for you and you hate that, don't you? Didn't little Miss Stanley make a fuss and say how you were misunderstood and how too bad it was? Didn't the rest of your friends pat you on the shoulder and urge you to be brave? That should have made your grief worth while."

"There's no use talking to you! I suppose you're going to make a martyr of yourself and sit up all night."

"I don't see why that should bother you. You'll sleep well enough. Nothing on *your* mind!"

Their whispers had been growing harsher and Terry stirred in his sleep. She bent over him to feel his forehead, smooth his blanket. She neither knew nor cared when Mark left the room.

The days seemed long as she lived through them, but April came with a sudden flash of forsythia and hyacinth that took her breath away. And Terry was so much bigger, so much more self-reliant, so much less a care. She could gauge the passage of time by him. By her reflection in the mirror, too, which told her that she looked forty instead of the thirty that she was. She creamed her face now at night, carefully, and tried to drink a quart of milk a day. Her mother was coming for a visit that summer. She had to look well and rested for that.

On a cool bright Monday toward Easter she discovered that the electricity had been shut off. At first she thought that something was wrong with the washing machine and then, when she found the lights wouldn't go on either, she decided that a fuse had blown. The utility company explained regretfully to her on the telephone that the current had been shut off for non-payment of bills. Perhaps Mr. Matthews had overlooked them, but it had been four months now. She put down the receiver carefully and felt humiliation crawling along her skin.

There was no getting in touch with Mark by telephone, because the laboratory stood separate from the other buildings and had no telephone service. She would have to go over there and tell him. Ann Milligan said that she would be glad to look after Terry.

"Are you sure you wouldn't rather have me zip over to your place to take care of him? Save you all that ride on the bus."

She dared not have Ann in the house. What if she should try to turn on the stove or make the oil burner kick on or wonder why the refrigerator was defrosting?

"No, I'll bring him there. It's awfully good of you, Ann. If it weren't so imperative that I see Mark—"

Ann was disapproving. "You going over to the lab? Oh, I wouldn't do that, Norma. Whatever it is, it can wait till he gets home, can't it?"

Naturally Ann would think this strange. Well, she couldn't explain. It would simply have to be chalked up as another count against her.

Mark was not at the laboratory. A Miss Collins talked to her instead.

"He came in but he went right out again. I think he had a golf date over at the club. If you'll give me your name—"

"No, it isn't that important. I'm a cousin of his"—she would not be cast in the comic-strip role of pursuing and avenging wife if she could help it—"and I'm just going to be in town for a few hours. I thought I'd like to see him."

"Well, he'll just be sick about it. Such a pleasant man, isn't he? I'd tell you to go on over to his house and wait for him, but—do you know his wife?"

"No, I—"

"She wouldn't be glad to see you, I can tell you that. She's a horribly bad-tempered woman. Seems a shame when he's so good-natured and all." She touched the arm of a burly man who was going by and explained the situation to him. "What shall I tell her to do, Mr. Randolph?"

He smiled at Norma briskly. "You don't happen to be the daughter of that uncle of Mark's who owns an interest in this business, do you? No? About Mark: leave word with Miss Collins here as to where you'll be about noon—if we're lucky he'll be back by noon—and just to make sure, better tell one of the other clerks who work with him."

"One of the *other* clerks?"

"Mr. Matthews is a clerk here, didn't you know? He can't be a technician because he hasn't a degree."

As he left, Norma said to Miss Collins, "And Mr. Randolph is—"

"Head of the lab."

She stumbled out into the sunlight and hunted a pay phone. As she waited for the country club to bring Mark in from the greens, her knees would scarcely hold her upright. How much did clerks make? How did Mark dare give his friends the impression that he was laboratory head when they might find out the truth any minute? Of course the firm was way out at the end of town, a little oil community that kept pretty much to itself, but there was always a risk. And how did Mark justify his membership in the country club out of a clerk's salary? Mr. Randolph had intimated that his work was unsatisfactory, that he was there only under the patronage of an uncle. When something happened to the uncle, what became of Mark then?

"What's wrong, Norma?" He sounded so anxious, so interested, that she knew he must have an audience.

"The electricity has been shut off because you haven't paid the bills. I don't care what you're doing, you get over there this minute and pay them. Borrow the money if you have to."

He said smoothly, "Yes, of course."

"I've been to the office. I told Miss Collins I was your cousin. You can ignore the message when you get back."

His voice was teasing, pleasant, but she knew what the men behind him would think. "Oh, checking up?"

"Good-by," she said wearily, and hung up. She had to stop shaking like this, had to pull herself together. Think of one thing at a time, that was the way to do it. Bus first. Take a bus to Ann's to get Terry.

She managed it, but afterward she could never remember how. What she said to Ann, how she got Terry home to his own back yard, when she changed into her house dress, at what time the washing machine began to work, all this was a blur and she was glad of it.

When Mark brought Mrs. Corcoran from the depot to the house Norma rushed out in the green June twilight before the car had quite stopped. Her mother's eyes were not strong enough to see her clearly, but her embracing arms felt a difference and she recoiled to put on her spectacles.

"You're so thin, Norma! What in the world have you been doing to yourself? You haven't been ill and not told me?"

"No, angel, I'm fine. Come on in. Dinner's ready."

At the dinner table Mrs. Corcoran saw, not the carefully arranged centerpiece, but the slight and constant tremor of her daughter's hands; observed, not Norma's smiles, but the hollows in her cheeks and the way she avoided looking at her husband; commented, not on the food, but on the state of things as she saw them.

"You look like a ghost, Norma. I can't get over it."

"She works too hard," Mark said. "I tell her to take it easy but she won't. Maybe you can do something with her."

"I'll make her take a good rest for the time I'm here."

In the kitchen she pulled Norma into a corner and put some money into her hand. "You're to buy yourself a new dress with this. Dad said so. No need to mention it to Mark."

"Really, Mother, I don't need—"

"You've never taken much from us. Sometimes I think we've let you be too independent. But *this* you're going to accept. So you might as well be graceful about it. I'll look after Terry and you can go downtown in the morning."

She had not known how badly she needed a holiday. It was unbelievably wonderful to have her mother get Mark's breakfast, to hear Terry's happy morning shouts from a distance and not have to run to see what they were about. She dozed until ten o'clock and felt like a traitor. But her cheeks were pinker and her eyes brighter than they had been in a long time.

The June weather was glorious and she hummed as she went downtown. Fifty dollars in her purse and not a care in the world! Her first glimpse of the downtown show windows affected her like champagne. The clothes on the stiff mannequins had colors as bright as fresh paint, stitched gloves lay in their cold hands, their slim feet boasted narrow exquisite shoes and delicately sheer stockings in colors she had never seen before.

At Miss Dalton's dress shop the salesgirl who waited on her was excellent, ransacking her stock cheerfully to find something that was not too expensive. They settled on a thin black with a rosy ruffled collar and pink pearl buttons. It was a twelve and it would have to be taken in at the waist.

"We can have it ready for you at three. If you're going to do some other shopping . . . ?"

"I'll pick it up on my way back."

She was pleased about the dress. She could hardly bear to watch it going away from her, its ruffles swinging over the salesgirl's arm. An extremely well-dressed woman smiled at her across the floor and Norma realized that it was someone she knew.

"Hello there," she called gaily. Funny she couldn't place the woman, there was something so familiar about her. One of her former customers at Klinger's? She racked her brains while the lovely creature walked toward her. It was impossible that she should have forgotten a woman who looked like that.

"I didn't know whether you'd want to speak," said the woman, "but it would be silly not to. Can't we have lunch together? I have to wait for a dress too and I haven't a thing in the world to do. We could find a quiet place and not set all the tongues in town clacking."

Rosemary! It was Rosemary Matthews, Mark's first wife, the one woman in the world she had never wanted to meet again! The shock made her feel cold.

"I—I have some other shopping to do. I don't believe I—" Rosemary stepped back quickly, as though she had been slapped, and Norma could not bear that. "I'll have a cup of coffee with you, though."

She dreaded the moment when they would face each other across a table, when the conversation would turn to Mark or to herself, but Rosemary kept chatting about trivialities, the steaming coffee was set down, and Norma's frozen blood began to circulate again. She found herself telling about the dress she had just bought and the things she was going to find to go with it.

"If I can get kid pumps, I can wear them right into the fall, don't you think?"

"Of course you can. And sheer black's good, summer or winter. I was looking for summer silks, something that I could wear at the office and that still wouldn't be too fussy to get the boys' dinner in."

"You're looking awfully well. I hardly knew you in that store, you seem so much younger somehow."

"I'm leading a sensible life for a change, taking care of myself. Enough rest. No worry. And I love my job. I didn't know how much I'd missed it till I got back to it."

"I've missed mine too."

For the slightest fraction of a second Rosemary's eyes rested on her old dress, on the thin face above it. "I suppose you have," she said kindly.

Rosemary was sorry for her! That was why she had asked her to lunch, because she thought that Norma could do with a bit of brightening up, a little friendly chatter. Surely that was the ultimate depth of humiliation, that your husband's first wife was not jealous of you, or triumphant, but simply sorry for you with a gentle unobtrusive pity. And it came to Norma in a flash that, just as she knew a great deal about Rosemary's life in what used to be Rosemary's house, so must Rosemary know a great deal about her for the same reasons. Rosemary must know to the fraction of an inch the worn spots on the living-room rug and how the recreation room had never been finished and how much the yard needed attention and the very things Mark said when he came in to dinner each night. Another woman would have been wickedly gleeful. Rosemary was too nice a person for that. She was, instead, sympathetic. And since she was the only person in town who knew Norma's side of the story, she came closer to being a friend than any of the other women could. Norma wanted to giggle. It was funny that your only truly sincere friend should turn out to be the one person convention demanded you should dislike or resent.

There was something she wanted to know and now she was not afraid to ask. "Why didn't the court grant you alimony? It seems to me you should have had it."

"Oh, the court was willing. I refused it." She looked at Norma apologetically. "I knew Mark would never get around to paying it, that there would have to be one mess after another about it. I didn't want that."

Norma said steadily, "I'm afraid people have been given the wrong impression about the alimony."

"One wrong impression more or less doesn't matter. As you should know."

"As I should most *certainly* know!"

They laughed together like two conspirators. They shook hands warmly before they parted.

"Good-by. Good luck."

"You too. Good-by."

The meeting left Norma in high spirits. Long afterward she knew that it was because, sitting at that little table with Rosemary, her path had suddenly become clear to her; she had gathered courage to shape her new life. But that afternoon she knew only that she was gay, that she hurried through the shops smiling to herself, that she gathered her parcels and raced home in the most excellent of humors.

For once she was going to look attractive at a bridge party. For once, with Mother there to look after Terry, she was going to be able to bend all her energies to having a good time. She put on the new dress with the rosy ruffle that hid the sharp collarbone and threw a flattering pink shadow on her face. She even pirouetted before her unkind mirror. Mark put his arms around her.

"Well, there's my girl," he said jovially. "Haven't seen you look like that in a long time. Why can't you always be pretty like this?"

Answers popped in her mind like corn over a hot fire. Because I don't very often have fifty dollars. Because usually I'm too busy taking care of my work and yours to have time to fix myself up. Because living with a man like you makes me too discouraged to care.

She gave none of them. She was past recrimination. Instead she pushed him away. "Let's go, Mark."

She had not intended to let him bother her, but when he threw open the Milligans' front door and called out, "Folks, meet the new Mrs. Matthews," she was suddenly hotly angry. She was tired of having her shortcomings thus subtly aired, she was sick of being the scapegoat. It was about time to fight fire with fire.

Smiling, she turned for their approval. "My mother gave me fifty dollars," she said. "Hence this splendor."

They got the implication, all right. She could see it in the way their smiles tightened. Well, it wouldn't hurt them to know that their precious Mark never gave his wife a dime, even if he did belong to the country club.

Amused, she watched how quickly they set up the tables. She saw that Mark had assumed his favorite pose, the drooping shoulders, the patient smile. She went over and slapped him on the back. "Buck up, old man. They're all sorry for you as it is. There's no sense in overacting."

Ann Milligan gasped as though a cold shower had hit her and began urging people to the tables. She put Mark as far away from Norma as she could get him. The tension eased.

But not for long. During the second round she heard Mark say something about his mother-in-law being at his house, saw the wry, persecuted little face he made when he said it.

She called over to him, "But it does save the price of a sitter, darling. Look on the bright side. When you don't have a dime, little things like that count. And of course it gives me a chance to get my hands out of dishwater for ten minutes." She looked about her, beaming. "Although there is a rumor about that I simply adore scrubbing floors and doing dishes, I don't like it any better than anybody else does. Isn't that peculiar of me?"

That shut Mark up. It shut everybody else up too. There was very little conversation until the supper was served at midnight. Then Bert Hanlon asked Mark how things were going at the lab.

Norma spoke first. "He's there so little, I doubt if he'd know. Have you been at the lab this week, dear? Things slacking off at the club?"

Ann was mad clear through. "Norma, stop it. You're being outrageous!"

"No, I'm just being honest. It's a new thing with me."

Sis Hanlon glared at her. "You're being another Rosemary, that's all. And we've had enough of that."

Norma pushed back her chair and stood up. She was cold and tired and trembling again. "You've hit the nail exactly on the head, Sis," she said. "I *am* another Rosemary." She turned to Mark. "Will you take me home, Mark? I believe their hearts will bleed even better for you if you're not here."

No one said good-by to her. They spoke, even to Mark, with restraint. Well, maybe she had thrown some doubts into their smug little minds. Not that it mattered.

In the car he said, "A fine performance. Let me congratulate you."

"I'm glad you liked it."

She was not angry with him, not any more. Looking at his weak pouting face, she knew that never again would he be able to raise any emotion whatsoever in her.

She let him take his coat and hat off and reach for his newspaper before she told him. "We're through, Mark. I'm going home with Mother and taking Terry along."

Strange that he should be surprised at that, considering all that had gone before. His face was blank with astonishment. "You're talking like a crazy woman!"

"On the contrary, I'm talking like a sane woman. At last."

"I won't give you a divorce. You have no grounds."

"Non-support."

"You'll have a hard time *proving* that!"

"Whether I prove it or not, all the dirty linen will at last be washed in public if you fight it. What your job is, how much you make, all the bills you owe. It will be very enlightening to your friends and you wouldn't want that, would you?" She stopped, surprised herself. "Why, that must be exactly the way Rosemary did it! You wouldn't have let her get away either, if you could have helped it." She laughed. "I'm beginning to think that Rosemary and I are twins."

"You weren't anything like her at first. I don't know what's got into you lately."

"I can tell you right now that your third wife will be just like Rosemary and me. You'll pick another woman like us, an efficient hard-working woman—naturally, it's the kind you need—and you'll give her the same treatment. And she'll turn out the same way."

He said with a catch in his voice, "I don't suppose the fact that I love you makes any difference at all."

She was careful not to sneer. "You don't love me. You can't love anybody. Love is being there when someone needs you. It's bending every effort to make someone happy. It's sacrifice and selflessness and—oh, there's no use. If you haven't understood it in all these years you're not going to now."

He stormed, he argued, he even wept. The only effect it had on her was to make her close the door into the hall

so that her mother would not hear and be disturbed.
When he threw himself down at her feet and put his head
in her lap, she was neither revolted nor touched. In the
mirror over the fireplace she saw the two of them reflected
—the tall thin woman in a black dress, the handsome man
with his head down in the classic attitude of lover's
despair—and the image held no drama, no personal con-
notation. She could look at it as though it were the colored
photograph of two strangers.

"Don't make such a fuss," she said gently. "I'm going
home and get a job and hire a housekeeper so that all
Mother will have to do is look after Terry. I hate to impose
on her but she *does* love me and she won't mind for the
couple of years until he's in school. We'll all be a great
deal happier that way."

"You don't love me. You never loved me."

"Mark, I—" She paused, choosing words that might
crack the hard armor of his self-concern and make him
understand a little. "Look at it this way: any sensible
human being has to ask himself what he's getting out of
what he's doing. What am I getting out of my marriage
that I couldn't have better without it? Well, there's Terry,
but you don't like him. You wouldn't want any more children and, with you feeling the way you do, I wouldn't
want them either. Outside of that, what have I? Uninter-
esting work instead of work I loved. Not enough money.
No peace of mind. No friends. No strength to lean on
when my own fails. It isn't good enough. Mark."

"But what about me?"

She hadn't made him see. There was no use trying.
Instead she laid her hand lightly on his hair. "Why, you'll

be all right. You'll find somebody else, and for a while you'll be very happy. Don't worry. There'll be somebody."

In her mind's eye she could see the Somebody Else, young, eager, ambitious, credulous, ensnared by the false pathos of this man. She shook her head and sighed a little for the Somebody Else. And as she raised her head she saw in the mirror that her face had already taken on a healthier color, that her brow was again serene, that her lips were smiling as though they could never stop. It was a face like that of a drowning woman who feels the dreadful entangling weight slip from her ankles and rises again to the glory of unlimited air. In time she might look as well as Rosemary had that afternoon.